# INSURMOUNTABLE

## SKYE CALLAHAN

VINCI

BOOKS

## By Skye Callahan

Vinci Books

vinci-books.com

Published by Vinci Books Ltd in 2025

1

The publisher and the author have made every effort to obtain permissions for any third party material used in this book and to comply with copyright law. Any queries in this respect should be brought to the attention of the publisher and any omissions will be corrected in future editions.

A CIP catalogue record for this book is available from the British Library.

Paperback ISBN: 9781036701819

# Chapter One

## SCAR TISSUE

### Miles

I NEVER STOOD A CHANCE.

Not once in my entire life did I ever know anything other than *this*.

Sex. Slaves. Drugs. Trafficking. Parties. Alcohol. Money. Extortion. Beatings. Blackmail. Pain.

And exquisite pleasure. Every fantasy at the snap of a finger.

"Miles," Gabe grunted my name as he pounded on my apartment door. I wanted to punch him in the face every time I heard his voice. Unfortunately, he worked for my security team—the most experienced dickhead I had. In more ways than one.

"New girls are here," he yelled.

New girls, or *fresh meat* as many of the men around the Retreat liked to call them. Everyone loves when the new girls show up. Clients, employees, especially the boss, Ross. I, however, dreaded the days when they showed up. The

1

men went wild, and depending on where the girls came from, I could have a near crisis on my hands.

Our organization was made up of multiple sex trafficking rings and brothels around the world. Some were high-class establishments with money to throw around on the girls. Expensive costumes, elaborate facilities, and medical treatment for the women. Others were more questionable, using drugs and violence to subdue the women.

Punishments. Rewards. The scales could tip drastically in either direction.

I snapped my keys onto my belt loop and opened my apartment door, walking past Gabe without so much as a word. He was an asshole. Pure and simple. An asshole who didn't listen to jack shit. And I was the poor, unlucky fool strapped with being his boss.

Most days he was lucky I let him live.

We climbed aboard the elevator and I punched the button for the fifth floor—The Commons—where we processed all the new girls.

"You're in a mood today," Gabe said.

I didn't look at him. If I did, I might have punched his smug face in. I straightened the collar and cuffs of my shirt instead. "I'm not in a mood."

When we stepped off the elevator, twelve new girls were standing in the middle of the room; blondes, brunettes, redheads, and everything in between. I assessed them all within seconds of laying eyes on them. The bold girls, the timid girls, experienced and unexperienced. It's always in their eyes, their posture, and their nervous twitches. They were all dressed in street clothes to make their transportation less suspicious.

"Take off your clothes," I said.

Some of the girls grinned as they pulled their shirts over

their heads and dropped their bras to the floor. Others simply did as told, keeping their eyelids lowered. They all obeyed without hesitation.

Major perk of the job—looking at all the beautiful women.

"You'll all be examined by our doctor." I strolled past the line of women, checking them each out from head to foot. "He'll make sure your birth control is up to date and you're in good physical condition."

I circled around the last girl and walked up the backside, checking out their other assets. The redhead on the end arched her back, pressing her ass toward me as I passed. Then she peeked over her shoulder and winked.

I knew she'd be trouble, but the patrons would fucking love her. A lot of the girls did anything they could to get their five seconds of recognition. They needed attention, Yearned for it. After all, attention was quite possibly the only thing they lived for.

But it wasn't that cheeky redhead that caught my attention. It was the willowy blonde in the middle. The girl with her hair falling over her face, struggling not to make eye contact. Struggling not to stand out. Not to be pulled aside or singled out. But everything about her made her stand out to me.

"You're first, Little Dove." I pulled her forward. "What's your name?"

"Alley." She lifted her blue-green eyes, peeking out from under her long, bright lashes.

"Follow me to the infirmary." In this case, being chosen first was not the worst thing. We all knew what would happen as soon as I turned my back.

The guards and men lining the back wall smirked at us as we passed, waiting for their opportunity to pounce. You'd think that eventually they'd get enough. They'd get bored. Obviously, they hadn't seen as much as me. Done as much as me.

Even new girls were boring.

But then, I'd been involved in this world for as long as I could remember. That's a long time to develop tastes and get your fill.

———

IT SEEMED like my days never ended, and, unfortunately, they blurred into weeks that also went on forever. I spent all day Monday processing the new girls and getting them settled with only a few minor incidents from my men. Tuesday through Thursday, however, I'd spent twenty-four hours a day merely keeping my team out of trouble. An impossible feat without new girls floating around. And Friday only meant it'd get worse. We had a hundred and six girls and ninety customers booked in for the night, starting at seven when we opened the girls. New girls, new visitors, and a security team with libidos of sixteen-year-olds meant my life would be a living hell until morning.

And then I'd start the process all over again.

At eight thirty—after having already dealt with enough crises to last an entire week, I pushed open the security room door, hoping for a quick update assuring me that all was under control. "Dig, what's the…"

The room was empty. The room was *never* supposed to be empty, especially on a packed night.

*Damn incompetent fools. Lazy bastards.*

All they cared about was getting their rocks off. Having their cocks fluffed. If replacing a single person didn't involve jumping through so many damn hoops, I'd replace them all in a fucking heartbeat.

I scanned the cameras. The lobby looked good. The grounds were fine. Every room. Every nook and cranny and foot of the yard. They're all monitored—at all times. More than two hundred cameras in the place that the security team are trusted to watch to protect our assets and our reputation.

In theory anyhow. Obviously, a flaw had developed in the system.

Some dipshits just couldn't take it. They got all hot and bothered and wander off to find an available girl for a quickie.

I scanned the third-floor rooms.

"Fuck," I yelled, slamming my hand down on the keyboard. The chair soared across the room, thumping against the back wall just as the door opened.

"Miles, I—" Dig stuttered. "I uh—"

"Shut up and call the team to room 329."

I bypassed the elevators—where any of the current customers would see me, and inevitably slow things up—and sprinted up three flights of stairs, ran down the hallway, and busted through the door of room 329.

The patron—a man I hadn't encountered directly before—was standing over Alley with his shoe in his hand, wailing on her. He was so busy with the beating that he hadn't even noticed that I'd entered the room until I had my arm around his neck. I twisted, throwing him off balance, and slamming him face first into the opposite wall.

"What?" he growled through his clenched teeth. "You stick me with a useless piece of shit then come in here to fuck me over?"

His shoulder jerked, but he didn't stand a chance of

throwing off a two-hundred-forty-pound, six-foot-nine man. "Don't even give me that. You don't rough up our girls and expect not to pay the price."

Finally, backup arrived, and I shoved the bastard toward Dig and Keith. "Take him to see Ross. I'm sure he'll have some ideas for getting a handle on the situation. Probably by kicking the shit out of him and sending him back to town with a one-of-a-kind warning. Ross kept enough shit to blackmail anyone, and if he couldn't find anything legit, he created it. "And Dig, be sure to account for your whereabouts when Ross is done with him."

"Yes, sir," he mumbled.

Alley laid curled up on the floor.

"Little dove." I brushed back her hair to check her injuries. Her lip was busted, and her right eyebrow bruised. The injuries I couldn't see were the most troubling. "Come on."

I lifted her up, but she kept her hands fisted tightly over her stomach and her eyes squeezed closed. "You'll be fine, Little dove."

When I laid her out on the exam table, her eyes opened, but she stared blankly across the room. "What happened?"

She narrowed her eyes and shook her head.

"Tell me," I coaxed, gently brushing her hair back. We only had a matter of time before Ross would finish up with the others and come in to pass judgment on her. "Just tell me."

"I don't know," she whispered.

Too many of our "partners" discouraged the girls from ever talking about the patrons, blaming anything that went wrong on the girl—no questions asked. "What did he ask you to do?"

"Nothing." Her voice shook. "He didn't ask for anything. Nothing. Nothing."

She cried, drawing her knees to her chest, and rolling to her side. "I'm sorry."

"Easy, Alley. Just tell me what happened. We have it on video, but I want your account."

"Why?"

If everyone else didn't get their jollies by fucking up the girls, my job would have been so much easier. They showed up thinking that everything I did or said was a fucking trap, and sometimes it took me months to get them to a point where I could work with them. I wasn't a softie, I just understood after years of experience that it was much easier for everyone if the girls worked with me, and for that, I needed some level of trust.

Unlike Ross, I didn't subscribe to the wasteful idea that every girl was replaceable. Technically it might have been true, but every replacement cost time and money. It didn't make business sense.

"I want to know what set him off," I whispered, squeezing her wrist. She shook but didn't pull away.

"He took me to the room. I looked up, waiting for him to tell me what he wanted, and he hit me. He said I was useless. That I couldn't give him what he needed, but he never...."

"Okay," I gently brushed back her long blonde hair to reveal her injured cheekbone. "I'm going to take off your nightgown so we can check your injuries. Can you sit up?"

She nodded, and with a little help, pulled herself up, so I could lift the nightie over her head. Her right hip and ribs were red, and she had a stripe across her collarbone.

"What hurts?"

Alley touched her side, then closed her eyes. "It's not that bad."

"We'll let the doctor make sure of that."

Her back straightened like I'd scolded her. "I don't need the doctor"—she swung her legs off the side of the bed—"I can go back to work."

I pushed her legs back onto the bed. She was holding on, but far too close to being broken. I wondered if it was already too late to pull her back. "No, Little Dove, that's not how we do things here. You'll get looked at and make sure you're all right."

She fidgeted and squirmed, so I helped her lie back down. "Sir, I feel dizzy."

"Lie back, Alley."

# Chapter Two

## IF I TREMBLE

### Alley

I WOKE up in a strange bed. The strangest of all beds. A large, comfortable, soft, and warm bed. In a private bedroom. All alone.

For a moment, I was horrified.

*What'd I miss?*

I remembered falling asleep in the infirmary waiting for the doctor, and then, nothing.

What had they done to me?

It had to be a trick. I waited for the punchline. For a group of men to walk in the room and take me.

I didn't move. Every breath was terrifying.

But the only thing that greeted me was silence. Utter silence.

No one to tell me what to do. No one to force me into sex. No one.

I had to wait until someone came to get me. Until someone came and told me what to do.

But then again, I had to pee. I had to pee so bad it hurt. So bad, I couldn't stand it.

I pushed the blanket back, careful to be as quiet as possible. Then, I swung my legs over the side of the bed and slowly stood up. Still utter silence around me.

I tiptoed toward the open doorway, holding my breath.

"Well, hello, Little Dove," the man who'd taken me to the infirmary said.

I gasped and dropped to my knees. "I'm sorry, Sir. I didn't—"

The next thing I knew his hands were on my arms, pulling me to my feet. "No need to apologize. How are you feeling?"

"I have to pee, Sir."

"Well, you can't do that on your knees. And I'd greatly appreciate if you didn't do it in my living room. Come on." He wrapped his arm around my waist and guided me to the next door. "Feeling better, Little dove?"

Why did he always have so many questions? Worse yet. Why'd he always act like he cared? I knew he didn't. No one did. Follow orders and fuck. That's all we were good for. "Yes, Sir."

"Then I'll leave you to do what you need to do."

He left me in the middle of the bright bedroom and closed the door behind him.

Odd. So odd.

I stared at the door for the longest time. Solitude. A private bathroom. More confusing than wonderland. I snapped myself out of my thoughts, finished my business, then faced the door down again. What could be waiting this time?

"Thank you, Sir," I said, lowering my head as I reentered the living room.

"Come here," he patted the seat next to him, and I obediently sat where he'd gestured. "Are you hungry?"

"Yes, Sir."

He nodded, pulling a blanket off the back of the couch and wrapping it around my shoulders. I stayed, frozen right where he left me, clutching the soft, warm blanket, but the warmth wouldn't penetrate my skin.

When he returned, he sat a bottle of water on the table and handed me a plate with two sandwiches.

*Two sandwiches.*

I wasn't sure I was capable of eating that much anymore.

It had been so long since I'd had more than nibbles here and there.

"Thank you, Sir."

As I ate, he dragged his fingers through my hair, gently separating the tangles and knots. It all played out like a strange dream. A twisted fantasy that couldn't possibly be my reality. No one had touched me with such softness in years—not without an ulterior motive.

I made it through a sandwich and a half before I felt so full that I couldn't possibly swallow another bite. Before I could apologize for not finishing the food, a knock on the door sent me to my knees. I curled up on the floor, clutching my hands in my lap and lowering my head.

I pissed off a client and now I'd pay the price. This was all just a ploy to make the punishment worse. To make me feel more guilty.

He put his hand on my shoulder, but the door still opened, and a set of footsteps approached.

"Miles, how is she?" I recognized the voice as the leader of this building. When you spend your time on your hands and knees, voices are as good as fingerprints. Sometimes I never saw their faces. I saw plenty of everything else, but I didn't want to see faces. I didn't want to associate their faces with my nightmares. And I definitely didn't want to see their eyes. Eyes are the worst. Dreaded, never-ending voids that only make false promises.

"You're interrupting lunch," Miles said with an air of disregard I'd never heard used toward the head of a house. They were gods—feared, revered, untouchable.

"I don't give a damn about lunch. I give a damn about accounts, income, the state of my affairs."

Miles snorted. "Well, this asset needs to eat and heal."

"The doctor said she's fine."

A frigid hand lifted my bruised jaw. I let him tilt my head up, but my eyes didn't follow.

"Really," Miles said. "Look at her. Who's going to pay for a bruised and beaten girl?"

He didn't know the men I knew. This had to be a trick.

"I trust you got to the bottom of the situation before you decided to bring her up here and pamper her?"

"I watched the tapes. There was no time for her to do anything before he started hitting her. He's a piece of shit with a temper. I pulled up his records. He's been arrested twice for disorderly conduct and investigated for domestic violence. He should've never been let through the front door."

"And whose fault is that? Last I checked, you were head of security. That's your damn job, but you sent him to me to clean up the mess—interrupting a perfectly good dinner with three of the new girls."

"Yeah, I order around a bunch of assholes who are more worried about which new girl they're going to fuck first. Every time we bring in new girls we have trouble."

"Then I suggest you crack down."

Miles groaned and stood. With one of them on either side of me, I felt like I was a baby lamb about to be ripped apart by two wolves. "How about I just replace them?"

"New employees are more trouble than new girls. You know that. Fix the problem before I have to. Makeup will cover the bruises. If nothing is broken, she can return to work tonight. We'll put her to work in the overlook where we can keep an eye on her."

*Work. Overlook.* I didn't know what that meant, but I didn't like the sound of it. The higher the man, the more sadistic he usually was. If the boss intended to keep his eye on me, that probably meant I was to be his for the night.

I hoped they couldn't see my hands quivering against my legs.

Fear would only feed their demented desires.

Miles stood, and Ross proceeded toward the door, leaving me on the floor in the center of the living room.

"Little Dove," Miles whispered, kneeling next to me.

*Don't talk. I'm not ready.*

The man had been right about me. I was useless.

I didn't even have enough in me to pretend anymore. The hope for escape had faded long ago.

"Alley," he squeezed my arm.

"Yes, Sir." *Focus. Stay alive.* The only thing that terrified me more than another endless day in this place—another endless month, year—was what they might do to me if I didn't listen. *Death.* A million possibilities worse than death. They wouldn't kill me unless it was their last resort.

But I was perilously close to that.

"I have a meeting in town. Will you be okay alone?"

*Alone?* I almost jerked my head up to see if I'd heard him right. "Here?"

13

"Yes, I intended to leave you here so you can rest. Unless you'd like to return to the Commons."

"No, Sir. I'd very much like to stay here." *What will I owe him for this?*

Brushing back my hair, he lifted me from the floor, carried me to the bedroom, and tucked me back in bed. This *had* to be a dream. An illusion of some kind. Maybe the concussion was worse than I thought.

"Do you need anything," he asked before leaving my side.

I closed my eyes and shook my head. How could I ask for anything?

———

ALONE IN AN APARTMENT. I had the whole place to myself. It was too good to be true. Too torturous to be true. The quiet was even more unnerving than the constant state of chatter and movement in the Commons. I shoved the blankets off of me and stared down at the bruises covering my sides and arms. It seemed like there were more than I remembered.

Miles hadn't said anything about how long he'd be gone, but the light outside the windows was already beginning to dim. It was only a matter of time before someone came to get me. Before I went back to work.

I slid my legs off the side of the bed, bracing myself against the mattress as I stood. My legs felt like stretched out springs, unable to hold their shape, and I put my hand against the wall to keep my balance as I left the bedroom and headed for the bathroom.

I turned on the water in the over-sized whirlpool tub, letting it run hot and steamy. Such a luxurious apartment. I wished I could let my mind go, float away just long enough to believe that it was mine. To pretend. Pretend I was a normal girl again. To pretend I had a future.

If someone walked in now, I could say I was getting ready. I could pretend to be the dedicated "worker." I'd put on the facade perfectly until last night.

What gave?

I reached for the medicine cabinet and pulled it open. How stupid was he to leave me here all alone?

A razor. That was all I needed. Anything sharp.

If all else failed. I'd take a knife from the kitchen. But I found just what I was looking for. I pulled the blade out of its holder. It all came so effortlessly. For once my mind was quiet, content. An exit. An escape. In the only way I'd ever get out of this. A better alternative than leaving my manner of death up to them.

I pressed the blade to my arm and a red dot of blood rose up around the tip. So beautiful. So freeing.

"Alley."

I jumped, pressing the blade to my palm. I must not have heard him enter because of the running water in the tub. How much had he seen?

Miles came toward me, but I arched my back, trying to hide my cut arm behind me. It was only a small cut. A nick. But now I was caught.

Whatever came next would be far more painful.

"Alley, give me your hand." Miles held out his own hand waiting for mine.

My breaths came so quickly that I bumped into the sink when a wave of dizziness hit me out of nowhere. And then I heard it. I felt it. A drop of something on the floor.

I followed the sound. Blood dripped from the hand holding the razor. No way of hiding it now.

Miles came at me and grabbed my arm, holding it out in front of me, palm side up. "Open your hand, Little Dove."

Why did he have to call me that? I relaxed my fingers, letting them fall open to reveal the tiny blade. He gently pulled it out of my blood-soaked palm and dropped it in the sink. Then he wadded up a wash rag and pressed it to my hand.

"Sir," I whispered, nodding to the tub. I didn't need more trouble.

He quickly turned the knobs without releasing my hand. I stared down at the bloody razor. *Almost. So close.*

"Alley." Every time he said my name it was like someone jerking at a chain around my neck. It pulled me back for just an instant and then sent me reeling even deeper. He took my other arm, turning it over to reveal the small trail of blood from the tiny gash in my arm. Without another word, he reached into a cabinet under the sink and pulled out a first aid kit.

*No. No. This isn't how it goes.*

He dabbed an alcohol pad over the wound, then pressed a band-aid over it. The other cut wouldn't be fixed so easily, but he took my hand with the same calm persistence.

I fisted my hand and pulled it away.

I didn't want to be fixed.

I sure as hell didn't want useless band aids covering the wounds.

Without warning, the tears fell, and my knees buckled.

Miles caught me, pinning me against the sink so I couldn't fall. "What's wrong?" he asked, brushing his fingers against my face.

"What's wrong?" I repeated. *What isn't wrong?*

I couldn't tell him. I couldn't say it. "Please, just kill me and get it over with," I whispered.

"Why would I do that?"

"He was right. I'm worthless. Bad business. It's what happens." It all came out. All I wanted was a quick end.

"Not here."

I shook my head, rattled with the sobs that built up in my throat and took my breath. "I can't. He was right. I can't do it anymore."

"Where were you before you came here?" Miles asked.

What did it matter? Who cared? "Milwaukee."

"How long?" His voice was so deep with an almost hypnotizing quality. It made me want to silence all of my thoughts just to listen, especially when he managed to stay so calm.

"Two years."

"Before that?"

*Why*? "Here. There. Everywhere." I'd traveled so much during the years before that, it was hard to tell where I'd ended up. "The last thing I really remember is Paris. Four fucking years of Paris.

"With Milo."

Out of nowhere, a bittersweet laugh rose out of my chest. *Milo. That damn bastard.* "If you don't kill me, he will." I finally lifted my eyes to his face. "Or your boss, one of the others. No point in keeping around a worthless girl."

"The guy last night had no right to say that or to lay a hand on you."

"No, he just has a right to fuck me." The overwhelming hopelessness had turned off my filter. "Just like the hundreds of other men. Only difference is he managed to see through me before he had the chance to take off his pants."

"Do you want to die?"

I dropped my head, shaking it subtly. "But I'm too tired to pretend."

He took my hand again and pulled away the bloodied rag. Most of the bleeding had stopped. And to be honest, the pain didn't even register. I'd endured more on a daily basis in some cases.

Miles took another alcohol pad and started at my fingers, wiping away all the dried blood, working closer and closer to the cut. "This will sting." He reached for a new pad and dabbed it over the cut.

"It doesn't look like it needs stitches." He pressed a gauze pad over it, then wrapped my hand with gauze, and secured it with tape.

"Why are you fixing me?" I whispered. If my eyes closed for more than an instant, I feared I'd pass out. My body had surpassed exhausted and this time, it wasn't letting me fight back, even if it meant life or death.

"Because I want to," Miles said. When he was done with my hand, he lifted my chin again. His hands were so large, enormous, and warm. "What if I keep you here?"

I shrugged, not really sure what he meant.

"What if I protect you?"

Protect? Against my better judgment, I lifted my gaze and stared into his eyes. I had too many questions to know where to start, and too many fears to risk it anyway.

"I'll keep you here," he continued, "In my apartment. You'll be mine."

"Why?" New tears burned at my eyes. I couldn't understand. I didn't trust him. What if he was far worse than any of the others?

If that was the case, why wasn't he punishing me now?

"Like I said, I want to." He lifted my arms up over his

shoulders, then wrapped his large muscular arms around me. We were complete juxtapositions. His skin and hair so dark, and mine so pale. His large muscular body and my tiny, skin and bones figure. His strength, my weakness. His confidence, my fear. "I like you, Little Dove. It'd be a pity to let you slip away and go to waste."

Empty promises and lies. "He won't let you."

"I can make a damn good argument when I want to."

"He wants me to work tonight."

"I'll take care of it."

Unable to fight it anymore, I dropped my cheek against his chest. So warm. Just like that bath I was currently missing.

# Chapter Three

## MONSTER YOU MADE

### Miles

I DIDN'T WANT to leave Alley alone again, but I had to make an appearance at dinner. I also had to figure out a way to explain her new injuries. Unless I could somehow manage to keep her hidden until she healed. Damn it.

As I buttoned my shirt, memories flooded in that I left long buried. I had been ten years old when I found my own mother dead in the tub. This was too close. Much too close of a call and much too close to history repeating itself.

Every day we saw the toll this place took on the girls. We had girls slip through the cracks or fall to pieces. I tried to make sure it didn't happen—it was the main reason I stayed—but with everything we demanded of them, sometimes the psyche just doesn't hold up. Too many others didn't care. If they did, we wouldn't stay in business.

It was a shitty logic, but the only way I had to explain my existence.

Alley's eyes were closed by the time I finished dressing, but I couldn't leave without one more thing.

"Alley," I traced my finger along her jawline.

It took her a moment to wrestle with her heavy eyelids.

"I need you to promise that if I let you stay here, you won't try to hurt yourself again."

She nodded.

"Say it."

"I promise," she whispered. "I won't hurt myself."

I kissed her delicate forehead, and when I stepped away, she looked on the verge of tears again.

"I'll be back soon," I said, patting her foot through the blanket.

———

"MILES, WHERE IS SHE?" Ross growled, taking me by the collar as soon as I entered the Overlook. He was smaller than me. Shorter, less muscular. With only a bit of effort, I could physically out throw him in an instant. But he was my boss.

My superior in title alone.

The thought made me laugh every time. As if I walked some moral high ground simply because I kept the girls fed and healthy.

"She isn't ready."

"That's not your decision. I gave you an order."

"And you gave me the job of looking out for the girls. She's hurt. You fuck with her tonight, and she'll be useless tomorrow."

"Fucking is what they're here for." He poked me in the chest as if it made his point more valid. "Don't go soft because one little girl actually gives you a boner."

"You want me to protect the bottom line or not? We have plenty of girls to go around—more than that. Protecting the long-term is more important than proving whatever point you're shooting for."

Ross huffed, whispered something to one of the girls serving drinks, then returned to his seat at the head of the table.

It worked for tonight, but I'd have to think of something much better to get him to agree to my long-term plan. Not that I'd be the first to claim one of the girls as my own personal slave, but Ross liked to keep them all in rotation. A concession that wouldn't be viable at the moment—if ever.

For all I knew she might be beyond saving.

I took my seat opposite Ross at the large glass table in the center of the room. The Overlook is where Ross liked to gather with all of his influential friends, clients, and sometimes key staff—usually me. With glass walls overlooking the rest of the twelfth-floor club layout and glass tiles in the floor that revealed specialized "play rooms" on the floor below, it was the only place to be if you wanted to watch every show—and every girl—in the house.

I truly wouldn't have been a bit surprised if one day he came up with the idea to add monitors to the ceilings connected with the guest rooms on the lower floors.

Nothing here was hidden, sacred, or truly safe.

Gabe sat at my left side with Kat, the new spunky red-head at his feet. Kat had the opposite problem of Alley—she couldn't keep her mouth shut and she enjoyed it all far too much.

Ross chatted away with the other two men who were seated at my right—each with a pair of slaves of their own for the evening—while two girls in pigtails and schoolgirl outfits served our dinner. Ross's VIP guests for the night were both rich real-estate tycoons like Ross's parents. I wondered if they knew what their only son had used their wealth and influence for, but as far as I knew, they were perfectly happy once Ross's wife popped out a couple of kids. A boy and a girl. On the outside, they seemed like the perfect family, but I only hoped that neither of his kids ever found out why he was never home.

Another of the slaves, Gabby, an olive-skinned girl with curly dark-brown hair, entered the room, circled the table, then dropped at my feet.

*Bloody hell.* I realize what Ross had been whispering about.

He raised his glass to me and winked, so I gave him a tight smile in return.

*Perfect.* Sometimes I had to perform as much as the girls.

Gabby nuzzled at the inside of my thigh and I picked up my fork. Whoever decided to combine sex and dinner was the true sadist of history. I cut off a piece of steak and fed it to her under the table. I didn't have an appetite. What I did have was too much Alley on my mind and a crabby mood to boot.

I could never stand having a problem that I couldn't fix immediately—looking it square in the eye and then walking away to let it set until I had time to return to it. Alley was that problem on steroids, multiplied by a thousand.

"I heard you had an incident here last night," Zeke said. He was the older of the two VIPs, probably by about ten years, and although he never wore his wedding ring at the Retreat, the tan line was quite obvious during the summer months.

I glared across the table at Ross. These were his friends and no doubt he was the one who'd brought it up. He didn't like problems, but he loved mentioning when he thought someone else screwed up.

"They were at my private party last night," Ross said. "I'm sure my hurried departure was hard to miss."

I raised an eyebrow. If only that situation had been as twisted and perverted as what I imagined. "Sorry about that. As you can imagine, folks around here get rather *excited* when we bring in new girls."

Ross was one of the biggest offenders.

Zeke gave me a sly smile and nodded his head. As he cleared the last bites off his plate, he adjusted in his seat pushing a girl's head between his legs.

During those moments, I wished the table wasn't glass.

Gabby nudged at me again, and with my plate nearly empty as well, my excuses to ignore her would run dry shortly.

I didn't usually have this problem, but with every clack of a fork against a plate, and every grunt and moan around me, my crabby mood grew even more. All I could think of were the increasing number of screw-ups and breeches. The tighter I pulled the reins, the more belligerent the security team grew, and if I even considered cutting them some slack, they were even worse than corralling a group of Kindergartners.

Their dismissive attitudes were due in large part to Gabe. He'd only been working at this location for two years, but he'd been with the organization for over a decade. Experience he used to throw his weight around, but the bad habits he'd learned along the way created a shining example for the other men to goof off. And the fact that he was sitting next to me, balls deep in Kat's mouth added a hint of bitterness to the mix.

He acted like a jackass and got rewarded at every turn

24

while I got the blame for his screw ups. He'd been the one in charge of managing background checks on patrons. Even if he delegated the duties, it was his responsibility to make sure it was done right. But he'd never give a damn.

I shifted in my seat to relax my back, forgetting all about the slave at my feet until she had her fingers at my zipper tugging it open. She'd misread my movement as an order, and if I pushed her away, Ross would have a fucking field day. So, I let her go, letting nature take its course while my mind worked a thousand miles away.

"You seem preoccupied," Ross said, yanking my thoughts back into the room.

"I've had a lot on my mind this week." I had wanted to tackle the obvious personnel issue again, but I couldn't go into any detail with VIPs in the room.

"Maybe," Gabe said between grunts. "You should relax," he grunted again, "have some fun, and get some sleep, instead of playing Mr. Invincible and working around the clock."

Gabby pulled at my dick and I stiffened.

Once again, all I could think of was Alley, particularly how I would have preferred her touch and her lips to this.

"You are a workaholic," Ross added.

"Thank you all." I closed my eyes for a moment, trying to reset my brain and return to the frame of mind that I needed to get through these nights. I concentrated on the adrenaline, the rush of arousal.

I felt the table shift and opened my eyes. Dessert had arrived, in the form of two girls coated in whipped cream, caramel, and chocolate sauce.

*Delightful,* I thought sarcastically.

They situated themselves in the middle of the table and began licking the sweet concoctions off of each other. Every man around the table came to attention—except for me. I'd seen it all too many times to really care and not even this little treat was enough to snap the sour out of my mood.

My muscles tightened as Gabby sucked harder, taking me deeper into her mouth, but then, Gabe stood and leaned over the table to lap up his share of dessert, and not even the physical sensations could save me.

———

ALLEY WAS STILL LAYING where I left her when I returned after dinner. I touched her neck, and she stirred.

"I don't want to get up," she whispered without opening her eyes.

"You don't have to. I'm going to take a shower. Sleep." I wanted to make sure she was still okay, but I couldn't handle crawling into bed until I was clean.

After I showered, I slid beneath the covers next to her and gave into exhaustion.

# Chapter Four

## COMING UNDONE

### Alley

THREE DAYS PASSED and Miles still hadn't asked me for anything. He gave me my peace and quiet, but aside for dinner when he went up to the Overlook, he stayed close by, gave me more food for a single meal than I was used to seeing in a day, changed my bandages, and checked to make sure everything was healing properly.

I couldn't get used to that kind of attention. I was used to gawking, grabbing, slapping, orders, and threats.

But the worst was the way he looked at me. The way it kindled the fallacy that I might still be somebody.

I curled up on the couch after lunch. He usually watched the news, then flipped the TV over to the sports channel. At least it gave me something else to pay attention to.

Miles's phone pinged, and he scowled when he looked down. "Ross wants to see us."

*Time for the end.* I always knew it was coming. I tugged at the hem of Miles's dress shirt that I wore. It was huge and soft, and comfortable, and best of all it came nearly down to my knees and covered my arms. It was the most covered I had been in years.

"Should I change, Sir?"

He stood, pulling me to my feet as well. Then, he tilted my chin up, in an attempt to force me to face him.

To face my fate.

"What do you *want* Little Dove?"

*Want*? That was such a dangerous word in my world. Freedom. I couldn't have that. Home. I could never go there again. My family was of the strict, one-way variety. They'd never accept what I'd done to survive. They'd only see that it was my fault.

"Alley?" he whispered in my ear and brushed his lips against my neck.

My thoughts—my wants—faded. *Always give them what they want*. "Whatever you want, Sir."

"No. I asked what you want." He kissed again, his lips on my neck, his hands on my waist.

*It's not real*. But if I could pretend, I could live in this illusion. "I want to stay here, Sir."

"That's all I wanted to hear." He pushed me into the wall and hoisted my legs up around his hips. He was so much larger than me that I couldn't even wrap my legs completely around him, but he easily held me, pinned there between his hot body and the cool wall.

His mouth captured mine, hot, demanding, insisting, but gentle.

*Fuck*, I had to concentrate. I couldn't lose it. I wiggled against him, squeezing his hips with my legs and pulling him closer. *Give him what he wants. Make it fast. Do your job.*

But every breath of his smell took my rationing away.

This never happened. Never.

*It can't be happening.*

Then, I remembered the message on his phone. "He's going to be mad if we leave him waiting." I feared Ross far more than Miles.

But Miles didn't stop kissing my neck or pressing his hips against me, pinning me harder against the wall.

"Pity," he mumbled. "I'm busy and haven't checked my messages yet. If he was in a hurry, he'd send someone down."

He sucked on the base of my neck right where it met my shoulder and I fell deeper under his spell. His hot fingers found the straps of my thong and snapped them, holding me to the wall with just his hips. Then, just as quickly he adjusted to hold me against him with one arm while he freed his cock and slid me down onto it. He didn't waste a second, filling me to the base of his shaft.

Impaling me to the wall. My eyes fell closed, and I pressed the back of my head into the wall as a loud moan vibrated out of my throat.

I could fuck any man they sent me to fuck. I could play my part. I could let my body go through the process—and most of the time, I did come. That was my job. But I never felt it. Before that moment with Miles, every sexual act had been purely a physical response to necessity and the right stimulation.

Every time Miles thrust inside of me, he filled me with a wave of ecstasy. In the same moment, it released me, showing me a new kind of freedom, and it confined me into a new and horrifying prison. One that existed based on hope and not fear. Hope was never grounded or reliable. He showed me a brand-new pleasure, laced with the fear that I'd never experience it again.

I dug my fingers into his muscular shoulders as he pounded me into the wall.

*A quickie.* Quickies were the best because often they meant an early end to the night. But this one, I didn't want to end. I wished I could sear every detail and sensation into my brain. The electrifying surge that pulsated through my core every time he sank deep enough in me to rub his pelvic bone against my clit. The stretch of him filling me. His hands squeezing my ass tighter. His hot mouth along my neck, jaw, and collarbone. The deep pants and groans in my ear.

"Oh fuck," the first unscripted words to fall out of my mouth in ecstasy.

He kissed me again, moaning into my mouth and plunging his tongue deep into mine until his taste overpowered my senses.

I knew only him. Only the binding force he built and stoked in my core.

"Come for me, Alley," he whispered, knowing that his permission was all I needed to let that force surge through my body. The orgasm came like a breached levy that had stood for far too many years against the floodwaters, pounding through every muscle and searing through my nerves with exquisite force.

It wrecked me.

Miles wrecked me.

He still held me against the wall panting against the side of my head, his arms curled around me, cock still inside of me. Then, he finally let me slide down to the floor, supporting me with one hand while he straightened my shirt and my hair. When I was righted, he pulled his pants back up over his hips, fastened them, and tightened his belt.

"I guess we should get to that meeting now," he said

with an ease that said this happened all the time. Just another everyday occurrence at the Retreat.

I didn't have even a moment to clean up before he pulled me toward the door and led me down the hallway to the elevator. I kept my head lowered as he swiped his card and pressed a button.

I had other things on my mind. Pressing my legs together in a useless attempt to stop the liquid running down my legs. There was no way it wouldn't be visible by the time we got to wherever we were going.

Miles pressed his mouth to my ear. "When we enter the office, you kneel next to me. Knees wide."

And that was exactly what he wanted. He wanted to show that he'd claimed me like a fucking animal.

*What if he's just using me, too?*

But if he'd agreed to keep me…. I knew that going through with this meant putting everything on the line. It meant putting myself on the line. Not like I did every other night. This was different. This made me vulnerable. It played to my emotions, especially with that dreaded hope. The hope that I might find safety with Miles. That I might find pleasure with him.

The fear that I might lose all of that just as quickly.

I followed him down the hallway to the end where he pushed open a door and led me into an elaborate office with a wall of windows behind the desk. Power. Freedom.

Keeping my head down, I sank to my knees, just as Miles had ordered, and waited for the judge to announce my sentence.

"It appears she's healed just fine," Ross said from behind his large, wooden, and elaborately carved desk. "Care to tell me why you haven't mentioned putting her back to work?"

Ross approached us both, but I couldn't look up—not only because I'd be going against my role. Even if he ordered me to look up, I'd be too embarrassed. That was a first as well. I could see the sparkling trails where the evidence of our quick tryst had run down my leg, and I wished that I could wipe it away or hide it somehow.

"And that's definitely not approved attire for slaves here."

Miles made a sound in his throat. "You know that bonus you brought up a couple of months ago."

"Miles, this isn't the time—" Ross began.

"You said if I got my planned system up and running and managed to save as much money as I had projected that I would get a bonus. Last I checked, the system is running *better* than projected."

"Fine, but—"

"I don't want money. I want Alley."

"You. Want. What?" Ross sounded like he nearly choked on his own tongue and then, I wished I could have seen his face.

"I want her. I won't be the first to have a personal slave, and right now we have plenty of girls to cover the business without her."

"You want your own girl, then go out and get her. Alley is bought and paid for. Property of the Retreat."

"As such, I'm forgoing the bonus you promised. I'm sure you'll find it to be an even trade. Unless you think Gabe can do my job to the same level."

"You've been here for nearly a decade, and you're threatening to quit over a girl? You're going soft, and that's dangerous in this business—not only *going* soft but being perceived as such."

"Believe me, boss, there's nothing soft about it. And with

my increased responsibilities, she'll be a bonus around the apartment. Stress relief, cleaning, cooking—"

"You really think that whore can cook?"

I had to listen to the entire exchange without reacting. Even though Ross was correct on the cooking part. They didn't really teach that in my line of work. I'd picked up a few things as a kid—grilled cheese, spaghetti, all the easy, mostly pre-packaged stuff—but I had only turned sixteen when Milo bought me. I had no practical life experience.

That was yet another reason I couldn't fathom freedom or anything else beyond this life, really. Eight years as a whore does strange and fucked up things to people. And to be honest, in that world, I was rapidly reaching "retirement". Everyone wanted young fresh girls, and that made me an old bag at twenty-four. Growing to even the ripe old age of thirty-five was beyond my comprehension.

"She can learn," Miles said. "It's not brain surgery. And besides, that'll be my problem, not yours."

Ross groaned and rocked back on his heels. Deliberating. Stalling. Thinking of a new argument. A new reason to keep his talons wedged deeply in my flesh and soul. "Seeing as we have a surplus of petite blondes at the moment, I'll agree, but you'll present her if ordered for any reason."

"Deal."

"They're all replaceable," Ross said in a light, lilting voice. Words I'd heard far too often. They sank to my stomach and made me sick.

"Come on, Alley," Miles said, dismissing his own boss and taking a step back.

Ross snorted. "Isn't that where you're supposed to argue that they're more expensive to replace?"

"What's the point?"

I stood, sneaking a look at Ross's face as I turned and

followed Miles out of the office and down the hall back to the elevator. His eyes were narrowed, and his mouth pressed into a line. A sudden surge of satisfaction came over me at the sight.

As the elevator doors closed, I felt a smile creep across my face. This whole situation was so unfamiliar. So strange. Miles was by far the most puzzling man I'd met in this world.

"What are you smiling at, Little Dove?"

He'd caught me. I bit my lower lip and backed away.

"Oh, no." He pressed a button, scanned his card, and the elevator stopped. "No hiding from me. Not after I just fought my boss for you."

He had. But I had a feeling it wouldn't be over so easily. Ross would have a comeback. If not now, next week, next month.

Miles pressed me against the wall, pinning my hands over my head with one of his large hands. Would he change now that I was his?

His other hand slid up my shirt, caressing the sensitive skin just below my hip bone.

*Focus. Remember your job.*

I focused on the only rule I'd ever had and never thought I'd need—don't fall for anyone. Falling meant eventually landing.

I pressed my hips against his, rubbing his erection through his pants. *Get him off. Get it done. Do your job. Concentrate, Alley, concentrate.*

Miles's phone dinged, and he smirked as he checked the screen. Then, he put it back in his pocket and raised his middle finger toward the back corner of the elevator compartment. Releasing my hands, he started unbuttoning my shirt.

"I need to borrow this," he whispered.

We were being watched. Not as if I wasn't used to that. But everything felt different with Miles. I couldn't detach. I felt it all. And it was dangerous.

Dangerous. Terrifying. And it gave me a rush.

Miles lowered the shirt over my arms, then pushed it up through a square in the ceiling, letting it hang down over the corner.

"Now then," he whispered, grabbing my hips. He took my right breast in his mouth, sucking and rolling my nipple with his tongue and lips.

I moaned, arching my back. I wanted more. For the first time. I wanted more.

*Your job. Your duty.* I kept reminding myself. I reached for the front of his pants, but once again, he grabbed my hands and pressed them against the wall.

"You're mine, Little Dove. Mine to do with as I want." He released my wrists and slid his long fingers inside of me. Rubbing my clit with his thumb he stroked me, pressing against the most sensitive nerve endings.

Every movement was slow and thorough. My eyelids fluttered, and I threw my head back. Then, his fingers left me. He traced my wetness up my stomach, then pressed his fingers to my lips. I opened my mouth, taking in the taste of both of us. Salty. Bitter. I sucked on his fingers until he pulled them free again. Then, his lips traveled down my sternum, across my stomach, following the path his fingers had left.

*He won't.*

My mind raced as he sank to his knees in front of me.

*Never.*

He lifted my left leg, putting it over his shoulder, then he pressed his mouth against my clit and sucked. My back arched with intense pleasure I didn't think was possible.

*Why?*

His tongue pressed at the bundle of nerves and he bit gently at it between licks and sucks. Then, his fingers slid inside of me again, pushing me faster and faster toward the edge.

*Torture*. The most pleasurable fucking torture I could imagine.

At the moment in life I thought I'd been stripped of everything I had, he'd given me something in a matter of hours that I never thought possible.

I screamed and bucked, clawing at his shoulders as the orgasm ripped through my consciousness and consumed my reality.

For a few seconds, the shuddering and gasps for oxygen were all that I knew. In one small moment, Miles had ripped my entire world apart. When I came back to reality, he was holding me up. His hands to my hips and my cheek to his chest.

"Thank you, Sir."

He pressed his finger to my lips. "I think that since you're mine now, that makes me Master, not Sir. But I don't intend to be thanked for doing what I please."

"Yes, Master."

"Now then," he whispered against my neck. "Tell me why you were smiling and why you hid it from me."

I didn't know what to say. "I—um"—my voice shook worse than my hands—"no one's ever." I swallowed. Why couldn't I find the words? I wasn't even sure what I was afraid of. "I've never seen someone stand up to the boss before."

Miles smiled and scanned his card again, sending the

elevator back into motion. "Life would be boring if I didn't."

A man bored in a sex retreat? Where he could have any fantasy fulfilled on a whim? How long did it take for that to become boring?

The elevator stopped, and I followed Miles back to the door to his apartment. After he closed the door behind us, I looked around the room. He'd mentioned cleaning, cooking, I didn't know where I was supposed to start.

"What do you need, Little Dove?"

"Where do you want me to start?"

"Start?" He snorted. "I have to leave for a meeting this afternoon. Have dinner ready by seven."

"That's it?"

He put up his hands. "Does it look like anything else needs done right now?"

I shook my head.

"You'll have to go downstairs to do laundry once a week. Keep the apartment clean. And make a list for anything we need in the kitchen. Aside from that, unless I ask you to do something, you're free to do whatever you like. The TV is hooked up to satellite."

*TV*? It had been more than eight years since I'd watched anything on television.

"I can pick up some books or anything else you might want. Is there anything you're interested in?"

I stood gawking for a second. "Nail polish?"

He smiled gently and stroked my hair. "I meant for fun."

"I—" I shook my head. Did he forget where we were? He couldn't have. "I don't know."

"Well, if you think of something, add it to the grocery list."

"Why?" The word slipped out, but my head was spinning, and I had to know.

"Because you can't just sit around here and twiddle your thumbs all day."

"No. Why me? Why are you doing all of this?"

"You intrigue me, Little Dove. You're a nice girl. Nice girls don't survive this and yet you have."

Nothing I'd had to do in the last eight years had been nice.

"You're a survivor," his voice softened, and he caressed my neck.

Why did every encounter between us turn me on?

"You're beautiful," he whispered, leaning over me and taking my earlobe into his mouth. "And I like the way you taste."

That final bit sent shivers down my spine.

"I have to get ready." He straightened, leaving me so suddenly, but he looked back and winked just before he entered the bedroom.

"Master? May I take a shower?"

"Of course," he shrugged.

———

AS I STOOD under the hot stream, I stared at the whirlpool tub. It seemed such a pity to not put it to use. I finished rinsing the shampoo from my hair, switched off the shower, and scampered across the tile floor to the tub. I let the water run hot, until the steam rose up out of it, and filled the tub until I could submerge my entire body under the relaxing liquid.

I floated there. Relaxing in the silence. Alone. Quiet. Protected.

There had to be a catch to this whole arrangement. More than cooking and cleaning.

But until that point, I wasn't any worse off than I'd been downstairs. This—even if it only lasted for a day or two—it was heaven.

I opened my eyes and saw Miles standing in the doorway wearing a black fitted T-shirt and a pair of jeans. The first man I'd ever encountered who could make my mouth water. I sat up, in a wave of panic—I hadn't asked to use the bath tub.

"Relax," he said. Then, he flipped a switch near the tub and the jets kicked on.

*Oh, my, god.* I sank back into the water. The jets massaging every muscle, and the sound of Miles laughter caressing my ears. "What's the catch?"

Why was I letting my mouth get the best of me?

"No catch. Do as I say, and I'll give you whatever you need."

Give and take. I had grown used to only experiencing one side of that equation. Every day men took whatever they wanted from me. They stole my energy, my mind, and my soul. Some of the overseers just gave us drugs to numb us and keep us under control. Some of them simply beat us into submission.

"You're not like the others," I whispered. Comparatively speaking, the girls here were treated like royalty. Granted, I'd only been there for a couple of weeks and I'd spent most of that with Miles anyway.

Miles sat down on the low wall next to the tub. "This world is all I've ever known. I watched it take my mother, and if I can help it, I don't intend on watching it take anyone else."

I mulled over his words. His mother was one of us? In

some of the Retreats, children weren't uncommon—but they usually became slaves themselves.

"I'd like to draw," I said, sinking chin deep into the water. "Maybe paint."

"Then, I'll get you some supplies."

*Too easy. It won't last.*

# Chapter Five

## SET ME ON FIRE

## Miles

HAVING a soft spot would get me killed—Ross had been right about that. I'd lose my position and the respect of the men I commanded. They could smell blood from a mile away and knew exactly where and when to strike. In a world where men get all the sex and worldly possessions they can ask for, power is the only thing left to fight for. And they all put up a damn good fight.

Especially Gabe. I couldn't turn my back on him for an instant without expecting to be stabbed.

And now, I had Alley.

She could potentially be a sign of my strength or weakness, depending on how I played it. I needed her on my side —I needed her docile and agreeable to my orders. If she questioned me, there was no way I could play this off as a power trip. But if she became the obedient, perfect slave, she could well be a testament of my growing power to the men below me.

But they couldn't think I cared about her.

Did I?

I cared about all the women more than was healthy. I couldn't turn it off. I'd experienced too much first hand. I'd almost become a slave alongside them. And if the women didn't last long as slaves, that was nothing compared to the life expectancy of a male slave. Milo would have auctioned my virginity off to the highest bidder—that is if someone else hadn't beaten him to it—and *he* was usually the highest bidder. I had a feeling that's what had happened to Alley. And Milo wasn't known for being gentle. Far from it. He usually fucked the girls up beyond repair on the first night.

The ones who survived were then carted off to his locations around the world or kept in his private stash.

*Enough thinking.*

I had a meeting to run. A meeting with all the dipshits who could easily be out to take me down, and I was about to kick it off with a bang.

"As of today, any member of this team caught fraternizing with the slaves—even in his off time—will face immediate and severe disciplinary action. Depending on my mood, you'll be demoted, transferred, or *dismissed*." The final option had a very different meaning in our world.

Gabe dropped his fist against the table. "You can't do that."

His complaint was one of a dozen others that echoed through the room.

"Quiet," I yelled, slamming both hands on the table. "I *can* do that. And I will. Unless you do your job, you're of no use to me *at all*."

"What are you going to do when you have no security team?" Gabe asked.

With a grin, I leaned over the table toward him. "I'll set

up my new team with a nice little break room adorned with your head on a mount."

Gabe snapped his mouth shut and sat back.

"If you think I'm kidding," I said, rising to my feet. "Consider how I got this job. If we have another incident like Friday night," I looked toward Dig, "I will fucking castrate whoever dropped the ball. Think about that as all the blood rushes from your brain and down to your dick."

Dig stood up. The gutsiest move he'd ever taken, but then I'd just cut off his favorite pastime. "You can't actually do that either." He looked around the table. "Come on, guys, Ross won't let him get away with this."

Everyone else sat in their seats, eyes down on the table. I shoved the table in Dig's direction, knocking him back in his seat, and before he could react, I darted around the table, pulled him to his feet and belted him right in the nose. "Meet the new *daytime* gardener."

———

I SMELLED something burning as soon as I stepped off the elevator. Alley's first attempt at making dinner, I assumed. At least she hadn't set off the smoke alarms. I would have never heard the end of that.

She waited for me in the kitchen where she'd plated one serving of food—a couple of fried chicken breasts, green beans, and bread. "There's more Sir—Master. I didn't know how much—"

"How about you put together another plate," I said peeking past her to see if I could figure out what she'd burned.

She pulled a plate from the cabinet, filled it with food, then turned and waited for my instructions. I pointed to the table across from where my food sat, and she rushed over and put it down.

"Have a seat," I said.

She bent her knees to kneel on the floor, but I caught her arm. "No, Alley. Sit with me at the table." I pulled out her chair, set out another set of silverware, and took my seat.

I took a bite of my chicken, but she sat and waited. "Eat, doll. This whole thing is going to get rather exhausting if I have to order you to do everything."

I had enough of that with my motley crew downstairs.

Contrary to my fears when I'd stepped off the elevator, dinner tasted good. A little bland for my tastes, but not bad for a first attempt. "I have to pay someone a visit tonight," I said, clearing my plate and silverware out of habit. "Be ready for me when I get home."

"What time?" she asked.

"I'm not sure," I said with a wink. I definitely had a new opening on my staff and an idea of who I might get to fill it, but I had to do some research first.

———

ALLEY WAS asleep on her stomach on the couch by the time I returned. Considering it was almost one in the morning and she'd had a long day, I couldn't blame her, but that didn't mean she could simply get away with it. I pulled out a small bag of sex toys that I kept in the top of the closet and sifted through the trinkets—clamps, plugs, rings, vibrators—until I found the medium sized plug. I squeezed some thick lube on it, making sure it was completely coated. I didn't want her waking up until I was ready.

Carefully, I pulled the throw off of her legs and inched

my hand up the back of the long shirt she wore. I really needed to get her some clothing of her own, but I got hard just seeing her in my shirts. Sometimes that was sexier than the most expensive lingerie.

I pushed the tip of the plug into her tight hole. She moaned quietly and shifted just an inch. So, I pressed it deeper, slowly teasing her with small, gentle motions.

Her breathing quickened as the plug slid into place, with just the base sticking out between her perfect little cheeks. I pressed at the base, so it wiggled slightly inside of her.

She groaned into the couch again and rolled to her side. I sat back, letting her move freely until I could determine whether she had woken. Her eyes remained closed, and her breathing even, although faster than normal.

I pushed her top leg until she rolled to her back. Her eyebrows furrowed for an instant, and then her face relaxed. I slid my fingers between her legs, stroking her sensitive clit.

"Miles," she whispered on a breathy exhale.

I leaned forward so my lips pressed against her ear. "Alley."

She startled and sat up as soon as I pulled away. "Master. I—" She squirmed, noticing the plug in her ass. "I'm sorry."

"Are you ready to take your punishment?"

Her head dropped forward. "Yes, Master."

I slid out of my pants and took a seat next to her, pulling me to her knees so that she straddled me. Her tight, wet hole taking my cock until her hips rested against mine. I rocked her back and forth a few times. "Then, I want you to ride me, but I don't want you to come until I say so. If you have to stop to keep from coming, I'm going to look in that bag and find a new toy."

"Yes, Master." She lifted herself and came down on my cock slowly.

"Faster, Little Dove." I moved her hips until she hit a rhythm and speed I liked—one I knew would quickly push her to the edge.

I watched her face tense every time she came down. It wouldn't be long. She moaned and her hips twitched and rocked erratically against her motions, and then, squeezing at my shoulders, finally her motions slowed.

"Keep up, or stop," I said, pressing at the plug in her ass.

She whimpered and dropped her head, stilling on my engorged dick. I felt every twitch of her struggle to sit right there at the edge and not come.

I reached into the bag and, although her head didn't move, I could feel her watching me. My fingers closed around a small chain, and I pulled it clear of the bag. Weighted nipple clamps. A perfect addition.

Her nipples were already erect and waiting, so I positioned one of the clamps over her right nipple, gave it a pinch, and then twisted the bolt to secure it. She groaned and twitched with the added sensation as I repeated the process on her left nipple. I released the chain to hang down, connected at the center with a small weight that would rock with her motions and pull on her delicate nipples.

"Again," I said.

She lifted herself and returned to the pace I'd set earlier, but I could already feel her struggling to stay in control.

I had to fight it too. I'd been waiting for this ever since I'd gotten her off in the elevator, and all the waiting and wanting was doing a number on my self-control.

After a long shaky moan, she paused again. Her tight opening spasming around me and begging for final release.

I reached into the bag again, but Alley closed her eyes. Instead of pulling out another toy, I dug the remote for the plug out of the side pocket and flipped it on high.

Alley screamed and jerked, taking my cock even deeper in surprise. The intense pressure and vibrations almost sent me over the edge with her.

"Fuck." She arched her back and looked up at the ceiling. Every muscle straining to stay in control.

I loved watching her like that. Seeing her realize that she couldn't fight me. She couldn't fight the intense sensations I gave her. I lifted her hips and pulled her down on me.

"Master?" she squeaked. "Oh, please, Master. I can't stop."

I forced her up and down—her light body so easy to manipulate however I pleased.

She tightened, holding her breath.

"Let it go," I said, pulling her close and pushing my dick deep inside of her. I just held her there as her climax did all the work, squeezing my cock until I came deep inside of her.

She dropped against my chest when the orgasm faded. I pulled out the plug, setting it to the side. Then sat her back so I could remove the clamps.

She groaned, pain pinching around her eyes as the blood returned to her nipples, and I pulled the throw from the back of the couch, wrapping up her quivering body and holding her close to my chest.

# Chapter Six

## DREAM FOREVER, NEVER

### Alley

HOLD ME.

All I wanted to do was be held. And suddenly there I was, wrapped in a blanket, exhausted from the most intense orgasm I'd ever experienced and curled up in his lap with his warm arms around me.

Even his punishments pulled me deeper under his spell muddling my sense of reality. The extreme culmination of emotions and endorphins burned my eyes with tears. Tears I refused to let fall.

*Never let them see you cry.* But Miles already had. He'd already seen me at my lowest and for some strange reason, he seemed to want to pull me back up.

Probably just to send me back to work.

But even with the doubts nagging at me, I couldn't resist him. He made me too weak. Weaker than I'd ever been. More vulnerable than I'd ever been. How long would the facade last? Days? Weeks? A month?

I couldn't fathom any time frame longer than that.

How could it be possible?

Miles carried me to bed, placed me under the sheets, and laid down next to me. So foreign. So strange.

I couldn't fight it. In fact, even though I knew better, I did just the opposite. I pressed my body closer to his, wanting his heat and comfort even though I expected rejection.

Instead, consistent with the conundrum he was, he rolled to his side and put his arm around me.

————

I SOMEHOW MANAGED to sleep so long that Miles cooked breakfast before I woke up—or maybe he just didn't want me burning the eggs like I'd burned my first attempt at rolls. Whatever the reason, he didn't mention it, he just sat a plate of scrambled eggs, bacon, and toast in front of me and dared me to apologize or ask permission to eat.

"Master," I scooped up a fork-full of eggs. "Can you get me a cookbook?"

"Of course," he said, chuckling.

"And some Miracle Whip." Why did my mouth always tempt me to test him?

Likely because he always let me get away with it. And so far, I had *enjoyed* his punishments.

He narrowed his eyes at me. "Okay. For what, may I ask, are you specifically requesting Miracle Whip?"

"My scrambled eggs."

He dropped his fork and folded his hands in front of him. "Are they that bad?"

"No," I whispered, hoping I hadn't actually gone too far

this time. "Me and Mom used to eat them that way. I miss it."

"Weird," he shook his head and went back to his own food. "But whatever you like, as long as you stick to the cookbook for *my* food."

I smiled and shoved another bite of eggs in my mouth.

———

AFTER WE FINISHED EATING, Miles went to the bedroom to get ready for another meeting. It seemed like he was always running off for one thing or another.

"You'll have access to the laundry room between one and five today," Miles said, straightening his tie. "I have things to take care of in town all day, and a security problem to straighten out."

*A security problem?* I frowned.

"You don't have to worry about it. Take the elevator down to the Commons."

*The Commons.* The first time I'd see all the other girls again.

"When you're ready to come back up, see Drake—he's the redhead who should be at the desk. Unless he's jacking around and making an ass of himself too."

"Yes, Master," I agreed even though the whole thing sounded quite intimidating. Instead of giving myself time to question it, I cleared the breakfast dishes from the table and filled the sink with hot water.

Miles came up behind me and kissed the top of my head. "I'll be home around six, but we'll be expected in the Overlook for dinner."

*Back to work.* I knew it couldn't last forever. Then, I

looked down at my clothes—another of Miles's shirts, a short sleeved grey t-shirt this time. "Master?"

"Little Dove?" he matched my light tone.

My heart thumped harder. Why'd he have to do that? "I need something to wear."

"That's taken care of as well. A delivery will arrive around noon." He held up a key on a silver necklace. "The door locks from both sides so you'll need this to get in and out—and to accept the delivery."

Miles dropped the necklace over my head and pulled out my hair from under it.

"Are you okay?" he asked, brushing his fingers against my jaw.

I tried to find words but failed and offered him a small nod instead. Freedom. Responsibility. Did he have any idea what that key meant?

———

THE DELIVERY ARRIVED JUST after noon, just as Miles had promised. It was like an out of body experience walking to the door, pulling the key from under my T-shirt and unlocking the deadbolt. But the lump grew in my throat as I opened the door to three strange faces. They looked me over for a second and I stepped behind the open door to block some of their view. The first man brought in an arm full of bags and placed them on the couch.

I thought there must be something wrong. Surely it didn't take three men to deliver a few bags. Then, the other two men carried in a dressing table, while the first left and returned with a padded chair that matched the table. After they carried both pieces of furniture to the bedroom, went back to the hallway, and returned with three more boxes and a dresser to match the table set.

*What the hell?*

"The rest is up to you, *slave*." With a lecherous wink, he handed me a slip of paper and they all left. I locked the door behind them and looked down at the paper.

*Have it organized by the time I get home.*

Organized? I looked at the clock. I had forty minutes until one when I'd planned on heading down to the laundry room to start the two loads of laundry I'd sorted out.

Nerves shook my hands as I reached for the first bag. Lingerie filled it to the very top—pinks, purples, blues— every variety and color. Nothing exciting to me, but I picked up all the bags and carried them to the bed so I could dump them out and sort them. Thongs, lacy boy shorts, skimpy skirts, teddies, corsets. Most of the girls downstairs would kill for such a haul, but for possibly the first time since I woke up in Miles apartment, I didn't feel a thing.

After I finished with the first bag, I dumped out the second—expecting more of the same thing. Lingerie was all we were ever really given. We either walked around in pieced together underwear or naked. The contents of the second bag scattered across the bed. *Pants*. I picked up a pair of long, soft, pajama pants. A light lavender pair, black, pink, red. I rubbed the soft material against my cheeks.

*Pants*. God, I couldn't remember the last time I'd slipped on a pair of pants, so I immediately pulled on the lavender pair, and folded the rest, stuffing them in the second drawer of the dresser. Next, I unfolded a stack of tank tops, T-shirts, and a thick robe that matched the black pajama pants. I pulled it on, too, over top of Miles' T-shirt, and proceeded to put the rest away. The final bag was topped off with socks, stockings, and underwear. I turned to stuff them in the next drawer of the dresser, but it rattled and jammed as I tried to open it. I shook it back and forth a few times until it finally slid open to reveal half a dozen pairs of stilettos. Not my favorite footwear, but I'd gladly wear them if I got comfy pajamas in return.

I scooped out all the shoes and lined them up along the top of the dresser, so I could put away the underwear. In the very bottom of the last bag, I found three pairs of pajama shorts and two pairs of jeans.

*Jeans. Where in the hell am I supposed to wear jeans? Miles really has lost his fucking mind.*

I put them away, feeling ironically like a real person for the first time in years. After all the clothes were tucked away in my new dresser, I brought in the boxes and sat on the floor to rip the first one open. I set up ten different bottles of nail polish, tucking them in one of the drawers on the dressing table. Beneath a manicure kit, I also found a large palette of eyeshadow, another with blush and contouring powder, concealer, a dozen sticks of eyeliner, twice as many tubes of lipstick, and a large pack of makeup brushes.

I organized everything away in the dressing table, and ripped open the second box, wondering what on earth could be next—almost like Christmas. A strange and perverted kind of Christmas. The light smell of perfume immediately wafted out and, on the top,, sat two bottles of perfume, wrapped in plastic, and beneath those, bath salts, oils, bubble bath, lotion, lavender scented shampoo and conditioner. I gathered up everything for the bathroom and ran through the apartment to place them next to the shower and bathtub, then skipped back to open the third box.

The third box was packed with a drawing pad, pencils, a

set of paints and brushes and a thick pack of canvases. Miles had kept his word. He'd made me his own and for the first time in eight years, I had someone to treat me like a human.

*You're still a slave*, I reminded myself. And I still had two bags of laundry waiting in the other room, but instead of doing anything, I just curled up on the couch in my robe and soft pajama bottoms, closed my eyes, and pretended that I was somewhere else where I didn't have a single care or worry.

---

AT ONE O'CLOCK I reluctantly pulled off the pajamas and robe knowing that I'd never get past the other girls wearing something like that. Instead, I put on a tank top and a pair of pajama shorts—it was close enough to a normal outfit for one of us. Then I grabbed the two bags of laundry and headed down to the Commons floor.

The Retreat felt so much larger when I had to navigate it on my own. It was as if I could feel the eyes of everyone watching me through the cameras and peepholes. I kept my head down as I passed the redhead sitting at the security desk just off the elevator on the Commons floor. It was his job to make sure none of us girls wandered into parts of the Retreat when we weren't requested. And supposedly to make sure that no one wandered into our quarters to get a freebie.

The laundry room sat at the back of the Commons room—where all the bunk beds and personal belongings of the girls were kept. Not that most of us had much in that category. When we were shipped to a new location, we were only allowed to keep the clothes on our backs. And then, we were only given what we might earn by sucking off a guard or giving a regular patron a fantastically good night.

"Look who's finally returned," Kat said, blocking my path. She'd been transferred in at the same time as me, and that was probably the only reason she remembered me. I'd only spent a few nights with the other girls, and they were so involved with their own cliques and business to notice the newbies.

"I was sent down to do laundry," I said.

A blonde girl came up on my right. "By your new *master*?"

"How'd you pull that off?" Kat asked.

"I don't know." I tried to keep walking, but four more girls helped them circle me.

"Share the secret, Alley. We all want pampered by a master for a while."

"Does he have room for another?"

"Who do we have to blow?"

The questions and smug comments came all at once like a freak traffic accident.

"Break it up," a male voice yelled.

I jumped at the sudden sound and looked over my shoulder to see Drake, watching us through the doorway until the crowd around me dissipated. I went straight to the laundry room and poured each bag of laundry into a washing machine. They were all fed the detergent and softener through tubes in the back of the machines, so I closed the lids and switched on the first cycle.

That left me all alone in the laundry room, terrified to go back out into the other room. I'd imagined it would be bad, but I thought I'd be able to find at least someone to chat with.

This was shit.

I sat down on the folding table in the middle of the room and stared at the washers as they filled with water and chugged through each cycle. My mind lost to doubts and worries until the door to the room swung and I jerked around to look back. Three of the girls who'd cornered me when I walked in surrounded me again.

"I'm just doing laundry and minding my own business," I said.

"Too good for us now, huh?" Kat put her hands on her hips and stared down her nose at me. She was one to talk.

"Of course not." So, now I had to take it from both sides. Perfect. Not quite the paradise I'd hoped for. And I knew it would only get worse during dinner at the Overlook.

The first washer buzzed so I jumped down from the table, intent to get everything moved over to the dryers and get back to the apartment as quickly as possible, but I only took two steps before something tightened around my neck. I grasped at the tight fabric, choking, as someone dragged me back to the table. One of the other girls grabbed my arm, helping the first pull me up and across the table on my back. Then, three more girls came into the room, restraining my arms and legs while I gasped for air. Kat put her hand over my mouth and held an index finger over her lips, telling me to be quiet.

I just wanted air. Oxygen. A breath.

The fabric around my neck loosened, and I inhaled sharply through my nose.

Kat stood over me, her face inches from mine until it was all I could see. "Such a lucky, lucky girl, aren't you?"

I tried to shake my head, but she held it in place. I didn't dare make a sound or draw the attention of the guards. It'd all only make the situation worse.

Backing away slightly, Kat held my head steady while

another girl pressed two strips over my eyebrows. They were thick and sticky....

*Fuck. Wax strips.* I struggled against all the hands holding me against the table and yelled against the hand on my mouth, but Kat jerked my head back, busting it against the table. Then she ripped off the first strip.

"Wonder what he'll think now."

"I thought we were just going to scare her," one of the girls said, loosening her grip on my ankle.

"Shut up, Lux, and hold her down." Kat ripped off the second strip. My eyes watered until I couldn't see the ceiling or the faces of the girls around me anymore.

"Kat, we're going to get in trouble," another girl said.

"You going to run upstairs and tattle to your Master?" Kat asked, yanking my hair again.

I shook my head, but how the hell was I supposed to explain it? He was going to notice.

Instead of releasing me, she gathered my hair, pulling it all above my head.

"Please stop. I won't tell him anything."

She pulled up a huge pair of scissors and started chopping at the handful of hair she held. Then, she pressed the blade of the scissors to my cheek. "He'll get tired of you, bored with you, and he'll come to us. Remember that."

I sobbed and curled up as they released me, leaving me alone again in the laundry room. The locks of hair they'd cut from my head laid on the table next to me. Unable to bear the sight, I shoved them off the edge of the table, into the trash can of lint. Then, I slid off the edge of the table and pulled the clothes out of the washer, stuffing them into the dryer as I caught my reflection in the window of the dryer door. No eyebrows. Fucked up hair. Nothing would fix this. And Miles would be pissed. Beyond pissed.

*What if he sends me back?*

*What if....*

I curled up on the floor next to the dryer to wait for the clothes, pulling my knees up to my chin and trying to figure out how to make all of this go away.

# Chapter Seven

## HAUNT ME

### Miles

"ALLEY," I called as I entered the quiet and seemingly empty apartment. I'd slipped away early when Drake messaged me that something went down in the Commons while Alley had been doing laundry.

The bathroom door was closed, so I tried the handle. Locked.

"Alley." I pounded on the bathroom door. When she still didn't answer, I slipped a pin into the hole and pushed the door open.

Alley sank down into the full bathtub until only her face remained above the water, half concealed by her messy hair.

Not messy.

I squinted at her. "What happened?"

A tear rolled down her face, and she slipped completely under the water.

"Alley." I reached into the water and pulled her above

the surface. She bit her bottom lip for an instant before a sob broke free. I pushed the hair out of her face and noticed that her eyebrows were gone, and her hair was half chopped off. "What happened?"

She shook her head.

"Did the other girls do this?"

She shook her head again, refusing to answer. We'd come so far, and suddenly we were back to this shit.

"Did *you* do this?" I knew she hadn't, but I needed her to give me *something*.

Again, just a shake of the head.

"Then, who?"

"I can't," she whispered. "I don't know."

"You can't tell me, or you don't know?"

"I'm sorry." She tried to slip away again, but I held tightly to her arm, making sure to keep her above water.

"If it happened on the Commons floor, all I have to do is pull up the footage. I'll know who did it."

"No," she sobbed.

I wished I could just drag the answers out of her. "You don't have anything to worry about."

"That's just the point."

I clenched my teeth. Nothing was more frustrating than trying to get answers from someone afraid to give them. Against my instinctual anger, I kept my voice calm and steady. "Start at the beginning and tell me what happened, Little Dove."

"They wanted me to know I'm not better than them. If you go after them, they'll blame me for that, too."

I ran my fingers through her wet hair and kissed her forehead. "They'll get over it, but I can't simply let them go."

The water in the tub was barely warm, so I released the plug.

"I'm not ready to get out," Alley said.

"You're going to turn into a very wrinkled Little Dove if you stay in the water much longer."

"Are you going to send me away?"

"You think I would have bothered to get you settled up here if I intended to send you away."

"It's only a matter of time," she muttered. "We're all replaceable."

"Don't fucking listen to Ross."

"It's not just Ross. It's every man who walks into one of these places. We're all the same. They're all the same. Another day. Another fantasy. We're just swirling around the drain waiting to get sucked in and never come back."

I hit the drain plug before the tub had emptied completely, but she continued staring right at the drain even when the water stilled. "You're not going anywhere."

"Just another fantasy. Do I look like your dream girl now?"

"You look a lot better than the women in my dreams." For the most part, they were usually dead. I didn't know how to convince her, though. Where this life had left off in tearing her down, the girls had picked up. Some of them could be as bad as our patrons, but then, that's exactly how they were molded and shaped. It's the only way they coped with this life. I couldn't even understand my own attraction to Alley. Why it pulled at me so deeply.

I'd been with more girls that I could possibly count. I'd brought them to my apartment, enjoyed them at parties, dinner meetings, in hallways, and corners. I started long before any man should—before I was even considered a man by most modern standards. I'd had a share of men, too. I'd been on Alley's side of things for a short time. After my mother died, they descended around me like vultures. I knew exactly the length certain men would go to get what they wanted. They didn't care that I was ten. They didn't care that I knew nothing of the world or how to fight for myself—or even that fighting for myself was possible.

But I still managed to find myself. Even in that impossible situation, I discovered a way to make myself useful. They manipulated me, but I caught on and manipulated right back. I learned the business. I picked up on languages and I learned about people—what makes them tick and what their weaknesses are. For the bosses, that was money and power. There was always more to be had, and the greedy bastards wouldn't leave any stone unturned. I found all the little holes and figured out how to seal them up until Milo couldn't help but take notice. He covered up my past —no one wanted to listen to the son of a slave—but he'd never make me forget.

Maybe Alley reminded me of the few memories I had of my mother. Maybe she reminded me of myself. Maybe it was the countless girls I'd had to carry out myself after drug overdoses, beatings, and suicide attempts. Maybe all of that was catching up to me and I couldn't turn away anymore.

I turned the hot water on, making sure it wasn't hot enough to burn Alley and let the tub refill. I reached over her to the back of the tub and opened one of the bottles of bubble bath I'd had delivered for her and dropped a cap full into the tub. Then, I stripped off my clothes and stepped into the tub behind her.

"You're mine, Little Dove," I whispered against the back of her ear. "Mine. Nothing anyone else does or says matters. If I wanted a temporary arrangement, I wouldn't bother with the furniture or clothes, I'd simply go downstairs and pick a girl out. Do you understand that?"

"Yes, Master." Her voice shook, and she refused to relax against me.

"I don't think you do."

She took a deep breath and leaned her head back against my shoulder. A small gesture, but at least she tried. "I wish I did. I wish everything didn't...."

"Didn't what?"

"I don't know. I can't make the thoughts in my head connect. Did you ever make those stupid paper houses as a kid—fold slot A into hole B? It's like that inside my head, except I'm missing the instructions to put it together."

"I think I get the idea, but no, we didn't really have toys where I grew up."

"Where was that?" she asked quietly.

"As far as I can remember, the Commons room at Boudoir Fetiche de Paris."

"You lived with...?" she turned to me with her mouth hanging open. "You...? But you're not—"

"I'm not a slave, no, but I lived there with my mother until she died. I don't remember much—seeing her with different men. Seeing all the women with different men. When I was ten, my mother killed herself. I found her."

"Is that why you decided to keep me?"

"I don't know," I answered honestly. "All I know is that I don't intend to let you go."

She let out a long sigh. "Then, I guess I need to figure out how to deal with the other slaves. I don't want to." She sank down into the water, finally relaxing against my chest. "I'm tired of it all."

"I can't take you off of laundry without making things

worse." The girls did all the laundry anyway—they were each assigned a day in the laundry room to keep them busy.

"I know. And if you track them down and punish them, they'll blame me for tattling. Whatever happens, I lose."

"Not anymore." I pushed aside her hair and nudged the side of her neck. "But for now, maybe we should address your hair. The hairdresser won't be back until Monday."

"Don't remind me." She groaned. "At least I have plenty of new makeup to draw on some eyebrows with. I think I can fix my hair—not like I can make it any worse."

I felt her take a deep breath, then tense. She turned and looked up at me with a strained expression.

"What's wrong?" I asked, taken aback by the sudden change in her demeanor.

She looked away just as quickly. "I forgot," she whispered, still so tense her body shook slightly. "I'm sorry, Master."

"What did you forget?" Judging from her reaction, I expected it to be something dire.

"My place, M—"

"Your place is where I tell you it is." I pulled her back against my chest, nibbling at the tip of her earlobe, then kissing her neck, while my hand explored her flat stomach.

"Your place is with me," I whispered against her neck. "And when we're here"—I squeezed her breasts, rubbing her nipples between my fingers until she arched her back— "like this. Alone. I don't expect you to hold your tongue or adhere to formal protocol. Understood?"

"Yes, Master," she said on a breathy exhale.

"Then, get dried off and see what you can do with that hair." I kissed her again. I'd find who was responsible and make them pay in kind, but I was useless in helping to fix hair, and if we didn't show up to dinner yet again, Ross would be the one handing down insane ultimatums.

"Are you going to pick out my outfit for the night, Master?"

"Would you like that?"

"Yes, Please."

"We're getting a bit formal again."

She gave me a faint smile but kept her head down.

Maybe I kept her because I wanted someone to talk. I wanted someone to take my mind off everything else—white noise in the background of my life. Someone as fucked up as me.

———

I LAID OUT A LACY, black baby doll top with a black bow just below the bust and the matching boy shorts with an attached garter belt on the bed and pulled out my own suit for the evening. I didn't even want to imagine what Ross had in mind for the night. It was always a show with him. It had to be. After seven years of working with him in one capacity or another, I still didn't understand how his mind worked. And I didn't want to.

At least I had some kind of excuse for my perversions—a weak one at best—but an excuse didn't exist for him. He was a rich socialite who'd had everything handed to him on a silver platter. Although, maybe that was the best excuse of all. His parents were real estate moguls who made their millions making—and sometimes breaking—high-dollar deals in business real estate. Thanks to them, he had a sense of entitlement that made Texas look puny. Unfortunately, he hadn't developed any business sense in the entire charade. He was headstrong, set in every idiotic decision he set his mind to and completely oblivious to the potential consequence, but usually, his shallow understanding of business made him easier to manipulate if I played my cards right.

I dressed in black for the evening—slacks and a long-sleeved button-down shirt—boring, but fitting for the situation. I had no desire to participate in Ross's theatrics but playing to his whims kept me on his good side. And I'd need that side if I wanted to convince him to let me restructure the security team. I'd had enough of their insolence, and Drake's failure to protect Alley in the Commons was only the topping on the cake.

Once dressed, I sat down on the edge of the bed, stretching my legs out and folding my hands behind my head to rest against the wall. I needed someone on the security team to help me crackdown—someone who cared more about security than getting his rocks off. Maybe someone who'd been castrated.

Alley peeked through the doorway, and I dropped my legs to the floor. Her hair now fell around her face in a long asymmetrical pixie cut that fell to her jaw in front and grew shorter and more layered in the back.

"You look beautiful," I said.

She paused, clutching the front of the thick black robe I'd had delivered.

*Beautiful.* It'd probably been a lifetime since she'd heard that word and longer since she'd believed it.

"I look like an eyebrow-less freak," she muttered.

I waved my hand toward the dressing table. "You work more magic like you did on your hair, and no one will be the wiser."

"My mom was a hair stylist, not a magician. I loved watching her cut hair." She sighed and sat down at the table, tracing her finger along the engraved wood that trimmed the surface.

When I thought of this place in terms of mothers, daughters, or sisters, I felt sick to my stomach. It didn't matter how long I'd been doing it. Or that I'd continued. I wasn't a complete heartless monster, but sometimes, I wished I could be.

Like I almost had been. The years I'd let the rage dominate. The slaves I took it out on. Every night I'd see my mother's face. She haunted me. Fueled the hatred. Until one day I realized that I was having exactly the reaction she would have hated. And then, I faced down two options—get the fuck out of the life and disappear or use my new found position within the organization to do as much as I could to protect the slaves.

I didn't even give a serious thought to the grandiose idea of setting them all free. That pie in the sky thinking didn't bode well with my overinflated sense of reality. Between all of Milo's clubs, retreats, whatever they might be called, he owned *thousands* of slaves in more than a hundred locations. He had more power and influence than the pope and more friends in low places than a cockroach. We'd never be free. None of us. Not his employees and sure as hell not the slaves. Following that line of thought merely became an exercise in futility and a path to depression.

I stood and popped my back, then walked over to stand behind Alley at the table. She'd already drawn on a couple of fairly believable eyebrows and had begun filling in the rest of her makeup. I pulled the collar of the robe down slightly to reveal her neck and pressed my lips against her warm skin.

"You're making this difficult," she said, wiggling away.

"That's the plan." I pulled her back and kissed her again.

"Oh, I thought the plan was for me to get ready for *work*."

The bench creaked when I sat down next to her, still toying with the edge of her robe. "Yes, but I currently need a distraction."

"Ah, so my purpose here is revealed." I could feel her trying to maintain the distance, so I pushed harder.

I brushed my fingers through her soft hair, watching it fall back into place. "What do you need?"

"To finish my makeup so I don't look like crap." She slammed her hand against the table.

"Impossible." I plucked the brush from her hand.

"Master, please."

She was flustered. So much so that the tips of her ears flushed. It made me want to nibble on her even more. "Tell me what you need."

Staring at our reflection in the mirror, she blinked repeatedly. "I *need* to not do this right now."

Seeing the tears well up in her eyes, I relented and rubbed her lower back, hoping that would calm her down. Then, I handed the eye shadow brush back.

"You're going to ruin me," she said, relaxing again and leaning over the table.

"Well then, just tell me one thing." I scooted closer, pulling her against me. "Is it worth it?"

"Being ruined?"

I squeezed the base of her neck and she dropped her head, moaning as I rubbed the tense muscles. "Yes, Master."

# Chapter Eight

## POISON & WINE

### Alley

THE RUINING WAS MORE than okay if he could make me forget reality for even a second. And I'll be damned if he didn't manage to do it with the slightest movements or the fewest words. How? I could never understand, but it comforted me and at the same time worried me.

His arms came around me, holding me against his chest. Exactly what I needed—and *feared*. I wanted to relax. To enjoy every second of a warm embrace, but my anxiety never rested. Hounding me like a hyperactive kid on a trampoline banging a pair of cymbals over his head.

I needed something to take it away. Just a momentary respite. God, I just wanted to get rid of the perpetual crawling sensation beneath my skin. The voices in my head that told me how dirty, useless, and hopeless I really was. The knowledge that I had no future. The fear that all of this would end as quickly as it began.

I took a deep breath and clenched my hands. "I need to finish getting ready."

I couldn't cry. I couldn't afford to mess up my makeup. It'd only set about a chain of mood swings that I'd never get under control.

I wanted to lose it. To scream and shout and tear through the apartment breaking everything in sight until the negativity was purged from my soul.

What if it had gone too deep?

What if the infection that brewed in me would never die?

"Look at me, Little Dove."

I opened my eyes—I hadn't even realized that I'd squeezed them tightly closed.

"Whatever happens, remember you're *mine*. You'll come home with me, and I'll make sure you're safe."

And just like that, everything broke, and the world went blurry. "Why? I'm nothing. I can't do this."

"Alley I—."

"You're just like all the others." I stood, pushing him away and stumbling across the room. "Why should I believe you?"

He didn't respond in anger, instead, he took my hands and pulled me to the bed, where he took a seat in front of me. "I don't have an answer for that."

"What'd you tell all the other girls?" I was certain there'd been others. That he'd done all of this before. I refused to let go of my suspicions, if I did, I'd fall too hard, too fast.

"All the other girls? What other girls?"

"Don't tell me I'm the first you've brought back here."

"Okay, you're not. I've easily fucked more women than you have men, but you are the first girl I've moved in here."

70

"Aren't you a Casanova?" *Stop, Alley. He's going to explode eventually, and you'll regret it.* But I couldn't stop the words. I couldn't stop the hate or the tears.

"How old were you when they brought you in?" he asked.

I didn't want to answer that. I didn't want to remember and I sure as this was hell didn't want to talk about it. I looked away. "Sixteen."

"Auctioned off?"

I wanted to double over and scream as the tears fell faster. I nodded.

"A virgin—"

"Please," I barely squeaked out the word, pulling away. Off the bed. Away from him. Away from the pain. Was he determined to break me?

"Milo took you."

"Please." I shook my head. "Please, Miles."

*God, I used his name.* My knees buckled, but he caught me and pulled me to the bed.

"How did you end up at the auction?"

My chest shook so violently I could barely inhale. "This guy, Aaron. I met him at a party. My friends had dragged me there because we all had a crush on the guy who threw the party. They ended up taking off with him, and I met Aaron. We… started hanging out after that. Getting high," I scoffed at my own stupidity. The tears had stopped with all of my emotion drained. "I must've passed out. I woke up in this tiny room. They kept me drugged until the auction."

"Milo's an asshole."

He said it so suddenly I had to laugh, even though it sounded more like a sob. "It's been eight years. I don't have anything left," I said.

"If I count back to the day one of the guards trapped

me in the bathroom of the Commons during a big party, I still have thirteen years up on you."

*Does he mean?* I froze, unsure of what to say.

"Milo lost his shit when he finally found out, but I eventually got back at all them."

"How?"

"By being smarter. I listened. Learned the languages, whatever I had to do until I had something to offer. It wasn't pretty and certainly never pleasant, but I eventually had enough to make Milo see I was more valuable as an employee than a slave."

"Noble." I scoffed. Deep down, I knew there was more to it, but I didn't want to see it. I didn't want to feel for him.

"No." He lifted my chin. Still gentle with every motion. How was it that he wasn't beyond pissed at me? Beyond tired of my falling apart? "It's Survival."

"I'm tired of surviving."

"I'm offering you something more," he whispered, pressing his forehead to mine.

But I still didn't buy it. I couldn't. *Wouldn't.* "Why me and not one of the hundreds of others who've passed through your bed?"

"You're not one of the hundreds of others."

"So, what? Save me and earn redemption?"

"No," he said, squeezing my hands. "I'm not deluded enough. I'm not long past redemption. In this case, I don't have all the answers. I was drawn to you from the moment I saw you. Then, I happened to walk into the empty security room and saw that man beating you. I carried you to the infirmary. I saw that distant look in your eyes, and it struck something in me. I can't promise you the world. No sandy beaches, white gowns, or happily ever afters. But I'll give you my bed and my protection, and I'll try my damnedest to make you forget everything else."

When he laid it all out like that, I felt my walls tumble so suddenly that my head spun. I closed my eyes and fell against his chest, letting his broad arms come around me and lift me to his lap. "How's my makeup?" I asked with a sniffle as I wiped away a fresh set of tears.

"Well," he looked me over, "I think the eyebrows are salvageable."

I laughed. "Great."

Even if he could just make me laugh every once in a while, I thought it might be worth it.

He wiped the smeared makeup and tears from under my eyes. "Luckily, we do still have about twenty minutes."

I sighed. I wasn't ready for the Overlook. For Ross, the other girls and whoever the hell else might be there.

"I'd try to get us out of it, but I need on Ross's good side."

"What will I have to do?"

"Likely, sit at my feet and look pretty." He kissed my temple.

"It cannot be that simple." I knew it, and when I thought of the possibilities, I wanted to vomit.

"Okay, then, while you're sitting there, come up with a plan to get the other slaves off your back while you're at it."

"Yes, Master," I mumbled, sliding off his lap. I rolled my eyes as soon as he couldn't see my face. He'd added yet another impossibility for me to worry about.

———

IF ONLY I could have imagined how right Miles had been. I followed him up to the Overlook, trying to keep my head down as we walked through the club-like atmosphere of the surrounding twelfth floor. Music pounded, colorful lights decorated the walls and floor, and crowds of men walked with drinks in hand and women at their sides or feet.

This was a place where almost anything went. No inhibitions and very few rules.

The Overlook stood at the center, a daunting structure of glass that, just as the name suggested, looked out over the entire club. The perfect place for a boss to spend his evening.

Miles didn't stop or even hesitate once as we navigated the floor and entered the glass room. He took the seat at the end of a long glass table, and I obediently knelt at his feet and kept my head down as the room filled behind me. Chairs scraped the floor, feet shuffled, and high heels clicked until the door closed and the room quieted.

I raised my eyes, hoping no one else saw my movement except Miles. He reached down and traced my jaw with his thumb, assuring me without words that he'd keep his word.

"Good of you to finally grace us with Alley's presence, Miles," Ross said.

*And it begins.*

*Miles will protect you.* I kept repeating to myself. I knew I could get through it. I'd done it before, but with emotions running so high the last few weeks, I found it more difficult than ever to compose myself.

Above me, the men continued to talk, Ross, Miles, and four voices I didn't recognize, and as the conversation drifted far away from me, my mind drifted as well. Throughout dinner, Miles slipped me little bites of food, and as they wrapped up the meal, the familiar sounds of sex rose up behind me. I looked up to Miles, waiting for his order, his cue, but he slid his chair away from the table and pulled me up into his lap. Out of the corner of my eye, I noticed that the sounds were coming from above the table where three other slaves, on their knees, had replaced the dinner settings and were now putting on a show of kissing, sucking, and licking each other.

Miles kissed my neck, drawing me closer as his hot breath hit my ear. "Up for a show of our own?" His words were only for me. I bit my lip and nodded.

He situated me so that I straddled his legs, and I unzipped his black dress pants, freeing his thick cock. With my back to the rest of the crowd, I ran my fingers down his growing erection and squeezed the head. His hands tightened on my ass, keeping me steady while his mouth explored my neck and the tops of my breasts.

I kept my eyes on him, my mind focused on every sensation until the rest of the club faded. It was a trick I'd perfected over the years. A way of shutting down the world so I could get the job done. But this time, I was shutting the world out of my pleasure.

Miles pushed the material of my shorts aside and guided his engorged dick into me. When I'd taken all of him inside me, he held me there, slipping my left breast from my top and sucking at it until I arched and squirmed with need. My hips rocked as much as his tight hold on me would allow as he bit down on the tip of my nipple, sending a rush through me.

His hands moved to my hips, and he guided me along his cock a couple of times to set the rhythm and motion. I held his shoulders to ground myself as I took over, matching his rhythm at first until endorphins clouded my mind. I could feel his eyes on my small breasts as they jiggled from the motions, so I arched my back, pushing them into his face. He took my hands, twisting them behind my back and holding them in one palm while his other hand moved between us, pressing against my clit until I cried out in ecstasy and slammed into him.

I rocked my hips harder. I wanted him deeper. Faster. He growled against my neck, and I felt my core begin to shake.

"Come with me," he hissed, and I let the growing tension in my core erupt into an internal firework show. My eyes were closed, shutting out the club, but I had my own lights show.

I caught a glimpse of half the table when Miles drew me against his shoulder. All eyes seemed to have been on us, rather than the scene Ross had organized, and I didn't give a damn.

———

AFTER MILES and I had showered, we curled up on the couch together, and he turned on some crazy police movie that did everything except calm my mind so I could sleep. I closed my eyes anyway, too exhausted to even try to make sense of the plot.

"I need stuff to make cookies," I said.

"Cookies? What kind?"

"Chocolate, for the other girls," I mumbled. "Chocolate makes everything better."

"So, you're going to bribe them," he chuckled, kissing the top of my head.

"Not a bribe. A peace offering."

# Chapter Nine

## BENT TO FLY

## Miles

ALLEY SKIPPED out of the bathroom and straddled my lap on the couch.

"I have eyebrows again," she said, wiggling them.

It had been two weeks since I'd sent her down to do laundry and she'd returned with her hair butchered and her eyebrows waxed off. I'd refused to let her go back the following week. She'd argued it, but I had been out of the building almost all week scouting a possible new recruit for the security team, and I wanted her to myself that day.

Or so it made a damn good argument.

"Really?" I brushed back her hair. "You call those eyebrows?"

She frowned and rolled her eyes. "You're an ass."

"That's my job." I grabbed the back of her hair—still too short to really get a good fistful—and pulled her against me until her lips waited millimeters from mine. Parted and ready. I could feel her breath on my skin and smell the sweet musk of her body wash. "Your job is to be beautiful and obedient."

"Wrong girl," she whispered, and I flipped her to the couch, pouncing on top of her as she landed.

I pinned her hands above her head and kissed the top of her exposed chest while she squirmed beneath me. She was learning to push my buttons, just as I'd set out to find all of hers.

I didn't make a habit of letting the girls get away with that shit, except for Alley. I wasn't about to drag her back down to that place where she didn't speak and nearly killed herself. I'd much rather have a mouthy, sometimes bratty, slave who kept me entertained. Pushing each other was a therapy we both needed.

She was a first for me in so many ways. A completely new experience in a world where those were few and far between.

I pushed my hand up her shirt, and she arched into my touch.

"Want to help me bake cookies?" she asked with a smirk.

"I bought you the stuff, isn't that enough?" The alarm beeped on my phone to remind me of the appointment I had in town. "Besides. I have to go."

I smacked her hip, then shoved up her shirt and kissed her stomach. "I intend to be back before you leave so I can keep an eye on things."

"Fine." She sighed. "Hope your meeting goes well, Master."

"Just stay out of trouble and remember that burned cookies probably won't earn you many friends."

---

I TOOK a seat in the back corner of a local coffee shop, taking a sip of the drink I'd bought solely to divert attention. At promptly ten o'clock the man I'd come to meet, Kirk, walked in the door. He glanced around the room, spotted me, then walked casually over to join me.

I'd been watching Kirk on and off for the last couple of months. Ever since our old supplier got picked up for being a moron and doubling in drug trafficking. One of my connections recommended that I make contact with Kirk and assured me that he could hook us up with any of the supplies we needed for the Retreat. While some things were just a few clicks away, others required some legwork, and that's where Kirk came in. His job was to save me time and trouble, and so far, he'd done just that.

As an added bonus, my supposed second in command, Gabe, hated his guts. I hated Gabe, his asinine comments and lecherous treatment of the women. He soared leaps and bounds over acceptable behavior—even in our profession because it made it impossible to trust him with any of the girls. Kirk had hinted that he'd be interested in a regular job and since we'd brought a regular doctor on staff who'd agreed to make arrangements for medical supplies, I considered bringing Kirk on staff as well.

Even if only to fuck with Gabe.

But I had a feeling Kirk could do much more than that. I knew people. I watched people. And my instincts were never wrong.

Kirk sat back in the seat across from me and crossed his arms. "I was surprised to get your invite. I figured following me around was more your style these days. I'm really hoping you have another job for me."

I pushed a manila envelope across the table. "You said you're interested in permanent employment."

"And you want references?" he said sardonically.

"You can fuck with Gabe all you like, jerk his chain, and get your jollies by pushing his buttons, but—"

Kirk put up his hands. "Just tell me what you want."

"I'm assuming you can do your homework and you know what I do."

"I know you go through an awful lot of medical equipment—or used to. Speaking of which, it's been a while since you've called on me. I was beginning to feel a little unloved."

I shook my head. What a sense of humor—no wonder Gabe hated him. "Well, I did do my homework. You cross me and you cross an organization that currently spans the world."

"In other words—" he drew a line with his finger across his neck. "I've done my digging. Everyone who's anyone knows about the Retreat. I hear it's the place to be on a weekend night."

"Some say it's the place to be any night." I flipped open the folder and tapped the first page. "Since you're familiar with the nature of the place, which of these men would you let in our doors."

He dropped his head, taking a moment to scan the first page. "No."

"Why?"

"Drunk and disorderly. Domestic disturbance. He sounds like a pain in the ass." He looked me dead in the eye, knowing he'd pointed out exactly what I'd wanted. He had gotten one right that my current team had let slip by, but the next shouldn't have been so easy.

Or so I thought.

Kirk flipped the page and immediately snorted. "No, again."

He'd picked up on that more easily than I'd expected. "Why?"

He paused. "I recognize the ink on his neck. Stitch's gang. Can't mean anything but trouble."

I scoffed and shook my head, thinking he might work out even better than I'd planned. "Maybe he's reformed," I said with a smirk.

"And you scoff at my humor." He flipped over the page and studied the next sheet. "No red flags. He has money to spare and no prior convictions, but I'm sure he has some dirty laundry somewhere to be dug up."

"Why is that?"

"No one who wants into a sex retreat doesn't. You don't just jump right into the deep end without learning to swim —unless you're a complete fool." He closed the folder and pushed it back toward me. "I'd make sure I knew something about that dirty laundry in case he gets ugly later."

"And what's your dirty laundry?"

He sat back again and shrugged. "You said you did your digging. What'd you find?"

"A few traffic violations and an assault charge for punching a drug dealer." The latter I certainly couldn't hold against him—in fact, I appreciated the sentiment behind it —but I wanted to hear his explanation.

He leaned across the table, his lips white with tension. "He was an asshole who tried to sell to my sixteen-year-old cousin."

"No qualms. We don't tolerate drugs on our property. Do you have a sister?"

You never really notice how much someone moves until he goes stone still. "I did."

*So, the girls might strike a chord with him.* "You sure you can handle working at the Retreat?"

"What do you want me to do?"

"You ever work in security? I need someone to help me watch over the girls. Make sure no one steps out of line and make sure no one gets inside who will cause trouble. We're in charge of everyone and everything that goes in and out."

"I did a private job for a while. Watching over my uncle's apartment building down by Waller Street. Until I punched a drug dealer, that is."

Consistent with every other time I'd encountered him, his answers were easy, not forced or unnatural, and he didn't fidget or search the room for answers like he needed time to consider. Rather, he seemed to say exactly what was on his mind. I liked him.

"You interested in the job?"

He narrowed his eyes. "Do I get to fuck with Gabe?"

"I'll pay you extra for it. But to be honest, your mere presence will do that. If you want the job, we'll be having dinner with the boss at seven tonight." I gathered the papers and stood. "Someone will be at your apartment to pick you up at six to bring you to meet me before dinner. Formal attire."

# Chapter Ten

## HELL HATH NO FURY

### Alley

BY THE TIME I finished the last batch of cookies, I felt like a baking expert. Four dozen cookies. It wouldn't feed every single girl in the building, but not all them would be in the Commons anyhow. After they cooled, I packed them all up in a plastic container and slid them down the side of a laundry bag. Perfectly disguised until I needed them.

Both of the bags were packed to capacity, and there was still dirty laundry in the apartment, but that was Miles's fault for not letting me do anything the week before.

Just as I was about to hoist them both up and be on my way, the apartment door opened, and Miles stepped in.

"Thought I told you to wait until I got back," he said, kissing my forehead.

"Not in so many words. I just want to get this over with."

"I'll be in the security room in case anything happens."

I smiled, but it didn't really make me feel better. I

needed to handle this situation on my own if I stood a chance of gaining any respect among the girls.

On my own I headed to the elevator, down to the Commons, and right into the group of girls who'd harassed me two weeks earlier. Again, I pressed a smile to my face, greeting them as I passed by and entered the laundry room. While I packed two washers to capacity, I heard the door open behind me and took a step to the side, so that I could see who had entered in the reflection on the dryers.

Just one girl, Lux, if I remembered correctly. She'd been one of the girls to question Kat as she ripped off my eyebrows.

"Didn't think you'd be back," she whispered.

"My Master needs laundry." I snapped the lids closed and switched on each machine. "You all aren't going to scare me off."

I picked up the laundry bags, feeling the weight of the cookies, and moved to the folding table—where I'd been when the girls had attacked me. I pulled the plastic container out of the bag and watched Lux's eyes widen.

"I'm not the enemy," I said, popping off the lid. "I don't want to be, and I don't think I'm better than anyone."

Quite the opposite, in fact. I'd been on the verge of breaking when Miles had taken me in—in my mind that made me weaker than the other girls.

Taking a cookie for myself, I slid the open container across the table. "Truce?"

"Kat will be pissed." She chewed on her lip for a moment, staring at the cookies. Then her hand shot out, grabbing a cookie and shoving it on her mouth. "Oh, my god."

She closed her eyes and slowly chewed.

"Good, I hadn't made cookies since I was like eight," I said.

Lux covered her mouth, laughing while she still had a mouthful of double chocolate chip cookie.

Two more girls came in, both carrying bags of laundry, but they each stopped as soon as they saw the cookies. I inched the container in their direction. They looked at each other, dropped the laundry, and each grabbed a cookie.

I didn't know either of their names and as well as I could remember, neither of them had been around the day I was attacked. "I'm Alley," I said.

One of them snorted. "Everyone knows who you are." She had jet black hair straight to her waist and beautiful golden eyes. "I'm Tryst, and this is Doll."

None of us ever used our real names, just the stupid names given to us when we were "acquired."

Doll waved but didn't speak.

"Doll never talks," Lux whispered. "And, I know a few other girls who'd love some cookies."

Her eyes sparkled as she waited for me to nod, then she darted out the door.

A *few* other girls in Lux terminology actually meant more than a dozen, and by the time I'd finished laundry, the room was packed with chattering girls snacking on the last of the cookies. They'd all introduced themselves and thanked me with the looks on their faces when they took a bite of chocolate.

I hoped that meant I'd at least have someone to watch my back if Kat went at it again.

When I folded the last of Miles's clothes, the door burst open one final time.

"What the hell are y'all doing?" Kat asked.

"Having a nice afternoon, for once," Tryst said, rolling

her eyes. She was standing next to me folding clothes and nudged me with her elbow. "Any way you can turn this into a regular thing?"

"I'll do my best."

Kat scowled at me. The cookies certainly hadn't won her over. I picked up the container—two cookies remained—and offered them to her, but she batted it out of my hand.

"Fuck off, Kat," Gabby said. Unlike many of the other girls in the room, she had been one of the girls who'd joined with Kat to terrorize me. She hadn't mentioned it, but dropping the whole issue was fine with me. "We all know that's what you're best at."

———

I GOT ready in the bedroom while Miles sat in the living room with some strange man who'd showed a little after six. Strangely, he'd seemed as surprised to see me as I had been to see him.

Ross had sent down a package for me, making me dread the evening even more—black high heels, a sheer black robe, and a bunch of chains and clamps. I had a feeling I was to be the main course rather than an observer this time, and why not since Miles and I had stolen the show last time?

I'd never win.

With my hair and makeup finished, I stared into the mirror. Miles entered the room, coming up behind me to squeeze my shoulders, then he leaned over me for a kiss.

*Maybe I might win a little bit,* I thought with a smile.

"Almost ready, Little Dove?" he asked.

I nodded toward the bed. He took my hand and led me to the bed, then he picked up the chains and took a seat in front of me. He drew my thick black robe open, and closed his mouth around my left nipple, sucking until I had to bite my lip to hold in my reaction. But what came next wasn't quite as pleasurable. He placed the cold metal over my hardened nipple and tightened until my eyes watered. Then he repeated the process on the other nipple. The chain between the clamps hung down in a Y, connected to a third clamp. The worst clamp.

Miles pushed my legs apart slightly, then slid his fingers between my legs, rubbing my clit until I could feel the tension build. Then, he took the third clamp and tightened it on the tender and sensitive bundle of nerves.

"How fast do you think we can get this over with?" I asked, dropping my thick robe to replace it with the sheer one Ross had sent down. Then, I strapped the black heels to my feet and did a little spin for Miles. Every movement nudged or pulled at one of the clamps, but all I could do was push the sensation out of my head.

When we reached the Overlook, Ross immediately intercepted me, taking my hand and leading me to the table. "Lie face down along the center of the table," he whispered into my ear. I lifted my knee to climb onto the table, but his hand on my shoulder stopped me.

"Oh, I forgot something," he said. Then a piece of lacy black fabric came over my eyes. "There we go."

Ross patted my ass, and I felt my way onto and across the table. The nipple clamps and chains dug into my skin when I laid down. Then, a pair of hands positioned my arms straight down at my sides. I listened for movement, trying to anticipate what might come next, but nothing could have prepared me.

Something hot dripped between my shoulder blades and I gasped. "Now, now," Ross said. "Our candle holder should really learn to be still. Something pressed into my skin in the same place where the hot wax had dropped. Another drip, lower on my back, then more pressure. A third just above my tailbone. Then, Ross pressed a candle between my thighs.

All through dinner, I counted my breaths to take my mind off the hot wax dripping and puddling on my skin.

I felt the fourth candle lifted from between my legs and hoped it was over, only to be shocked out of my hopeful place as new drops of wax fell along the backs of my legs, all the way down to my ankles.

My concentration broke for an instant, but I reigned it back, continuing my count until the last plate was collected and all the candles were finally removed.

But that wouldn't be the end of it.

"Roll over," Ross ordered.

I rolled, and the once hot spots on my back and legs pressed against the glass of the table.

I felt a finger move across my stomach, slipping under the chain and pulling it up until it tugged painfully at my nipples and clit. More hands moved me, placing my palms up, and then a cool glass was set in each of my hands, followed by more glasses on the table up against the outside of my legs and one next to each shoulder.

"New guy," Ross said. "What's your name again?"

"Kirk."

"Ah, new guy, perhaps you'd like to remove the left nipple clamp."

The clamp jostled a bit, and I tensed. I knew what was to follow would be simply excruciating.

"Now, Alley," Ross spoke again. "Be sure not to spill our drinks. If you do, you'll owe a blow job to anyone who so much as loses a drop."

*Fuck.* Even though the blindfold still obscured most of my vision, I closed my eyes and prepared. The first clamp loosened and in an instant, blood rushed back to my nipple.

I gritted my teeth and screamed but didn't move an inch. Another pair of hands immediately loosened the second nipple clamp. I couldn't stop the tremor that swept through me, but I managed to contain it enough that I didn't feel a drop of liquid on the table.

One final clamp, and I knew Ross would do the honors. Fingers probed between my legs. One twist to the clamp. Pause. Another twist. Pause. One final twist and the clamp was free. I pressed my hips into the table.

*Do not move.*

My eyes rolled back in my head for a second as I fought through the pain. Once again successful not to spill a drop. I'd overcome the challenge, but that hadn't been Ross's plan.

After everyone removed their drinks, he grabbed my ankle and pulled me to his end of the table until my ass sat on the very edge. He jerked off the blindfold and leaned over my face. "Impressive. No wonder Miles was so quick to snap you up."

I didn't respond, knowing it would only egg him on.

Ross lifted his glass to his lips, then paused, held out the red liquid and lowered it above my face. "Open up, Alley."

I obeyed, and he poured the bitter liquid into my mouth. "Don't miss a drop," he hissed continuing to pour.

My mouth filled quickly, and I had to choke down the liquid that just kept coming. Once his glass was empty, he reached for a wine bottle.

I wanted to shake my head. I wanted to look to Miles for help. But I didn't dare take my eyes off of Ross or disobey him.

He tilted the bottle, pouring the stream once again straight into my mouth. I tried desperately to balance swallowing and breathing as the continuous stream of musty liquid fell against my tongue.

"Enough," Miles said, shaking the table with his objection. "You know her body won't be able to handle so much alcohol so fast."

Ross growled and slammed the bottle against the table. "Remember your place."

"I'll never forget," Miles growled back.

I was helplessly caught between two posturing men.

Ross leaned over me again. "I think your Master needs a drink."

He filled my mouth with wine, then nodded toward Miles. I rolled to my hands and knees and crawled across the table. When I reached Miles, I placed my mouth over his, allowing the liquid to pass to him. He took it all, and licked a drip from my bottom lip, then pulled me into his lap where Ross couldn't get to me again.

But Ross had already done his damage, and as the alcohol rushed my system, I fought to keep my eyes open.

The next thing I knew we were back in Miles apartment on the floor of his bathroom, while I puked so violently that I saw spots before my eyes. Miles pressed a cold rag to the back of my neck, but my anxiety rose with every wave of nausea.

Finally, I got a break and pressed my cheek against the cold tile wall.

"I need to run upstairs," Miles said. "I'll be just a few minutes."

I couldn't imagine what might be so important, but then, I was also too weak to argue.

# Chapter Eleven

## CHANGED BY YOU

### Miles

AFTER I RAIDED THE INFIRMARY, I returned to Alley in the bathroom. She hadn't moved much from where I'd left her, so I hoped the worst of the vomiting was over.

"I'm not the greatest at this," I said taking her left arm and looking for a good vein. Luckily, she had a large one near the surface. I tied a tourniquet around her arm, wiped it with alcohol and prepared the needle.

"What are you doing?" she moaned.

"You need fluids." I pressed the needle into her skin, hoping for a flash of red to show I'd hit the vein. Slowly, I pushed forward. *Come on. Come on.* Then finally blood appeared, and I released the tourniquet and pulled the needle free of the tiny line. When the IV was set, I pushed through a syringe of saline and taped it in place.

"It burns," Alley said.

I kissed her forehead and attached the first bag of liquids. "It'll be much better than dehydration."

Squeezing the bag, I forced the initial fluids into her body. Then, I scooped her up and carried her to the bedroom, jerry-rigging the bag to the headboard to keep the saline flowing.

When she finally fell asleep, she tossed and turned every few minutes moaning and grunting. I wished for something I could do to ease her misery, but we both had no choice but to wait it out.

At nine o'clock, my phone rang, showing Kirk's name on the screen. He'd helped me get Alley back to my apartment without incident after Ross had finished his show.

I snuck away from the bed, to avoid waking Alley and accepted the call.

"I'm in," Kirk said.

I scoffed. "I figured we'd scared you off last night."

"Close." He exhaled. "You need help. I'll do it."

My shoulders finally relaxed, and I rubbed my hand over my mouth. "Good. There's a furnished apartment ready for you here. I need someone who's readily available."

"Today?" he asked.

"Today. Can you do me one favor on your way over here? I'm in need of chocolate cake."

"Chocolate cake, huh? How's Alley doing?"

"She could be better or much worse. I've been pushing fluids through an IV, and she's sleeping it off." I peeked into the bedroom again. "She informed me a couple of weeks ago that chocolate fixes everything, so…." I trailed off, not knowing where to go next. Or if I needed to justify my request to him.

Considering the state he'd seen us both in the previous night, I doubted there was much left for me to hide. If I hadn't had Alley to take care of, I might have ripped Ross's head off then and there.

"Got it," he said. "I'll be there soon."

"Then, I'll make the necessary arrangements." I let out a long breath after I disconnected the call. For once, I had a good feeling. A confidence that Kirk would help me continue the changes I wanted to make, help me crackdown on the team, and most importantly, protect the girls.

Protect Alley.

## Alley

By the time I woke up, it was nearly noon. My head felt heavier than a concrete truck, and my tongue had taken on the texture of a felt blanket at some point in the night. Miles had already removed the IV, so I rolled out of bed, and stumbled to the living room, hoping to find him.

"Morning, beautiful," he said.

I knew he was wrong. And yet, I knew he meant it. I had finally realized that he'd never said anything he didn't mean. I collapsed on the couch next to him and curled up against his side.

"Hungry?" he asked.

I moaned. Even the thought of food made me sick. "Not really."

"What if I have chocolate cake to offer?"

I sat up so I could see his face. "Are you serious?"

"And ice cream." He winked. "Chocolate fixes everything, right?"

*How'd I get here?* Even though I'd lived it, I couldn't process the fact that I'd gone from rock bottom to *this*. "I'm not sure it fixes a hangover, but I'm willing to give it a try."

Maybe I didn't have everything I wanted. Maybe I'd never have my life back, my freedom, but I had Miles. Two mismatched people in a far from perfect world.

Some people would never understand.

They'd never see my life as anything except a disgrace, but the magic of it all—the only magic I needed—was that he saw me as more. More than a slave. More than sex. In our quiet moments alone, we had each other. No matter what the rest of the Retreat threw at us, I had his one promise...

*No sandy beaches, white gowns, or happily ever afters. But I'll give you my bed and my protection, and I'll try my damnedest to make you forget everything else.*

vinci-books.com/skyshedevil

**I traded my badge for leather, my heels for boots, and my old life for the Devil's Pointe MC.**

One wrong move, one slip, and it's all over. I need to live, breathe, and bleed their world if I want to survive.

Turn the page for a preview…

# She-Devil: Chapter One

## GONNA GET MINE

### Brooke

*One day, when they least expect it, I'm going to make them all pay.*

I barged into the loft office overlooking the biker hangout below, closing the door behind me with a resounding thud. Sawyer, the President of Devils of Ashville MC, stared down at the notebook on his oversized, engraved desk refusing to raise his head to acknowledge my ruckus.

I marched toward his desk, planting my hands on either side of the notebook full of his chicken scratches. "I want to go on the run."

Sawyer raised his left hand and waved me off, but I refused to move. "I've earned it. I'm as qualified as anyone here."

If not more. For the last ten years, I'd worked twice as hard as any man here to earn my place in the club for half the respect. And although I didn't really care about the run up to Utica, if I didn't demand to be included in club business, Sawyer would happily leave me in my office downstairs, processing alcohol shipments and ordering pretzels. I'd fought for my position as Club Treasurer, and as a fucking officer, I insisted to be treated as such.

Sawyer expected this run to be pivotal in consolidating our power over the local drug networks since one of our biggest allies and rivals, the Gold Family recently destroyed themselves like a stressed-out snake turning to cannibalism. I didn't give a damn about the external politics of it all. Didn't give a damn what people chose to pollute their bodies with or the quantity or quality of said pollution, but as the only patch-wearing officer without a dick—I grew tired of being the last to know and least likely to be included in club business.

"Why can't you just settle down and become a good Ol' Lady?" That was Sawyer's only concern. We all knew he'd only been humoring me and trying to relieve the thorn I'd plunged in his side when he finally agreed to let me join the boy's club. There were two types of women in my world, Mamas or Ol' Ladies. As the daughter of the Club's President, I was expected to conform to those misogynistic ideologies, but neither of those revolting titles were the least bit appealing to me.

I held a growl deep in my chest. Men could get away with violence. They could yell. Throw things. Flip tables. Hell, it was expected of them, and it all sounded rather appealing, but female violence was "unhinged," "hormonal," and made me a liability. No one ever said making it in the boy's club would be easy. Where they relied on violence, I wielded restraint. Quiet, conniving, and well-hewn restraint.

Sawyer continued to write in his ledger, his personal

hall-of-fame for fucked up deeds. "Vin has been asking about you."

*Gavin.* I shuddered at the thought of him and tasted a rancid acid in the back of my mouth that reminded me of his cologne.

Spook, Vin, Dodger, Bull; they all asked about me because they saw me as a power move. Not because they liked me—most couldn't stand me, and I gave them a good reason for it. Gavin was the worst of the bunch, giving into entitlement and throwing his power around from the moment he became Sergeant-at-Arms. He and his crew only cared that by topping me, they might win Sawyer's favor and take my position as Treasurer.

I cleared my throat. When I wasn't doing exactly what Sawyer wanted, he preferred to ignore my existence, but I wasn't walking away from this.

Finally, he looked up. "I have a meeting at one. Caine is bringing in our new Prospect."

His eyes narrowed on me, knowing how much I hated hang-rounds and Prospects. I suspected part of him also hoped that some new guy would show up who could finally put me in my place for good.

"Maybe you've seen him around Bone Grinders the last several weeks. Cannon says he's been real useful."

The heat of anger climbed up in my throat as I studied Sawyer's expression. I plastered a sardonic smile on my face. "Is *he* going on the run?"

Sawyer didn't answer, but the deadpan look he gave me was answer enough.

"You're bringing in a fucking Prospect to do a run when you have someone perfectly capable standing right in front of you? I did earn this patch." I leaned over his desk, pointing at the Treasurer patch on my cut. Sure, I could run all of the club accounts above and below the table while managing our hangout, The Pit, but no one cared about that. No one cared about all the time I spent keeping the heat off our activities. The state of my genitals meant far more than my rank. They'd all prefer me to lie on my back and let a man with a quarter of the knowledge, an eighth of the intuition, a sixteenth of the experience, and one-hundred percent testosterone take my position.

Sawyer let out a long breath and picked up his pen again. Since I was fourteen, I'd been a cog in his master plan to expand his gang beyond the borders of Devil's Point. A bargaining chip. A distraction while he clawed his way into new deals and took out the competition. That was the only worth a daughter held in my world. Sawyer thought he could beat me down, steal my power and force me to comply, but he only taught me how to use sex to get what I wanted.

The urge to flip his desk over on top of him grew, but our private conversation was cut short when the door to the stairwell opened and two men stepped in. I straightened, standing next to Sawyer with my arms crossed over my chest. Caine glanced at me, the same quick, passing glance we always shared when trapped in the same room, before setting his gaze on Sawyer.

Caine had been around as long as I could remember. We'd grown up together. Me; Caine; his wife, Thea; and my brother, Dixon. My dead brother. Caine was a few years older than me, but at least six inches shorter—more when I wore heels. Of all the people here, he'd once been my friend. That changed shortly after we buried what was left of Dixon's body three years ago. Now, everything between us centered around these awkward and frequent encounters.

His companion's eyes lingered on me and I waited for

his initial reaction. Typically, they fell into two categories: the smirk at the laughable idea of a female officer, or a lusty-eyed stare that completely dismissed my rank. But he kept a straight face, letting nothing slip by.

"You're early," Sawyer said with a ragged, clipped tone. No, he wasn't a man of punctuality, but he'd use any tool available to make sure the person standing across from him remained at a disadvantage.

Caine fidgeted, looking at his watch. "We can wait until you're done. I had one and didn't want to be late."

"It's twelve fifty-seven," Sawyer said, eyeing me, but I didn't move. If he fought me and I dug in, I'd make him look the fool, and he knew it. Sure, he'd eventually win and get his way, but he wouldn't want to give the new guy any ideas that he had trouble controlling his officers. I had learned a few of his tricks.

With another glare, Sawyer pushed away the papers in front of him and sat back in his chair. "Trent, right?"

We got hang-arounds like other people got stray cats. Usually they came and went when things didn't happen on their timetable. But Trent had been working steady in the garage—on our above the board work—for a couple of months. Mainly a gopher, but I'd heard Cannon bragging about his work over drinks in the bar.

I tried not to pay more attention than that to any man who showed up—most of the wannabes were worse than the patches. A girl with a patch caught their eye and suddenly they thought, *one fuck and I'm in*.

But now this name on payroll became a real threat. Competition. It was a sad and pathetic statement on my position in life when a patch-wearing officer had to look at a Prospect as competition.

Prospect stepped forward with a nod but stayed silent.

Caine had obviously instructed him to answer questions and nothing more. His dirty blond hair was pulled back into a stub of a ponytail, and he held Sawyer's gaze with his golden-green eyes. He wore a thin black hoodie with the sleeves ripped off and my gaze moved down to his bare arms.

Bare wasn't a just description when nearly every inch of skin was covered in ink from his knuckles to his shoulders. Sharp lines. Patches of color. Smooth details that joined each image in utter perfection. I followed the designs back up to his shoulders and noticed fragments above the V-collar of his shirt, stretching up his neck.

So many details.

I wasn't a fan of men—or people in general—but I could stare at a good tattoo for hours. Apparently, some people do that in art galleries, but it's not the same. Tattoos are intimate, living manifestations of a person etched into their skin. Love. Lust. Desire. Our deepest yearnings and fears revealed, even if neither the wearer nor observer fully understood the meaning of every detail.

My largest piece of art was still in progress. Soon, it would cover my back and wrap around my ribs. I itched for more. Especially standing there staring at his pieces.

*Tattoos are better than sex.*

I wondered how many more tattoos he might have hidden away, but questions and thoughts like that were bound to be misunderstood, interpreted as an ulterior motive to inquire about other things. And if I didn't stop staring, someone would notice.

I wrestled my attention back to Sawyer. He'd been quiet far too long, leaving me to wonder what he was thinking. That was a doorway into lunacy I wanted to avoid.

*Is he suspicious?*

We were all suspicious of newcomers, but Sawyer... Some days I'd call him paranoid. Reckless the next. Careless the following. And sometimes it changed hour-by-hour or minute-by-minute. That was one of the ways he maintained his power and authority—always being unpredictable and turbulent.

*What is he plotting?*

Caine shifted his gaze, first to me, then to his friend before Sawyer finally relented. "Who have you ridden with?"

Trent's stare didn't waver. "My uncle taught me to ride before...." He glanced down. "He was with the Brothers of the Wheel until they dissolved."

"Dissolved?" Sawyer laughed. "What a political way of putting it." He lowered his tone. "They were slaughtered, worse yet, it was someone on the inside."

Trent grimaced. "I've been laying low. Hard to move on when there's no one to trust and no family to fall back on. My uncle always wanted me to join BOW, and working in the shop with Caine and Cannon has given me a piece of that brotherhood he always spoke of. Ignited my hunger for more."

He was good. So good, I almost puked. Somewhat believable, but no one around here said what they meant. Laying out all your cards was always a bad idea. If you didn't keep secrets close to the vest, first you lost your edge, then your life.

Always have a backup weapon. Never lie to a brother, but guard your secrets, and equally important, guard everyone else's. I excelled at the secrets game, after all, that's the only way I managed to get a patch in this male-dominated circus.

"Well, Trent, are you up for a run?" Sawyer asked. His voice lost that grating, barking tone.

My eyebrows shot upward. *Mother fucking incredulous jackass.* From the look on his face, I guessed he made the offer just to screw with me. But I couldn't believe the rat bastard would choose a Prospect over me for such an important run.

Then again, I could believe it. Not like it was anything new.

I had to bite my tongue. *Pick your battles*, I reminded myself. *Choose the situation and audience with care or the punishment will be far worse.* I had to carefully balance what I intended to gain with what I would certainly lose, and this battle wasn't worth it.

*One day.*

*One day...*

"Yes, sir." Trent smirked. "Anything you need."

Too eager. I would make this Prospect's life a living hell. Much as I enjoyed admiring his ink, I swore that one day I'd rip out his tongue and wipe that look off his face with it.

"Brooke," Sawyer barked my name, and I jumped, losing my thoughts. He turned to me, and I didn't trust a bit of that glint in his eye. Then, he glanced back to Trent. "Prospect, this is my daughter. You'll take a little trip up to the Salt Grove and follow her lead."

*What?* I straightened. *Just the two of us? What is he planning?*

Oh, I had a feeling I knew what he had planned, and my stomach turned over on itself.

"He can't be running around like that." Sawyer gestured toward Trent. "Get him a leather out of the storage room."

Sawyer flicked his wrist for Caine and the Prospect to leave, and after they stepped out, he turned to me. "Lonnie owes me. Make sure he hasn't forgotten. Either get me pictures or cash."

*Pictures?* "You want me to break his legs?"

"You want me to treat you like one of the boys, so I don't suggest complaining," he said flippantly. "None of them would have a problem with turning to violence. In fact—"

"Yeah, I know. Enjoy inflicting the pain, but I suspect there's more to this."

Sawyer cocked his head, turning one eyebrow up in apparent amusement. "Ah, yes. Initiate the Prospect. Get inside his head and find out his secrets."

He nonchalantly returned to his work as if I was his personal secretary and he'd just asked for a cup of coffee. But it all made sense. I stood there, shaking my head. No matter what I did or the number of times I bailed out my so-called father or so-called brothers, my usefulness in his eyes came down to one thing. "That's the reason you're not sending him with one of the boys? Of course, you wouldn't ask one of them to do that."

"We all have strengths and skills," he mumbled. "It just so happens that your unique contribution to this club is between your legs."

*Damn you.* It was the only thing I wanted to say, but even those words weren't strong enough. I bit the inside of my cheek as my breathing became more ragged with each passing second that I shared air with that rancid man.

"And besides...." he continued, but I already wanted to vomit on his face. "Even if I did ask one of the boys to fuck someone—and let's face it, I have—they don't complain."

My lips curled, but I fought down the retort begging to break free. *Right, because you're god in this twisted world.* He didn't have to mention that one of those times he'd asked the boys to fuck someone, that someone had been his own daughter. He and I knew that, for the most part, he gave the boys license to do exactly as they wanted.

"Lonnie's wife will be home from work in two hours, so you're running out of time. Deliver the wake-up call. Then, how you handle Trent is up to you."

"Want me to take a picture of that, too?" I snapped. It was a stupid move.

I heard the pen in Sawyer's hand creak with increased pressure and inwardly shrank back. I wouldn't let him see me cower though. He expected this club to break me, but I refused to bow down. Not after everything I'd risked getting this far. The first time I told him I wanted to join, he laughed. The second time, when I'd actually done my homework and brought him information I knew he'd been trying to get his hands on for months, he beat the shit out of me. The third time, when I dared to mention my demands in front of the other members of the club, he let them deal out the blows. He thought I'd crash and burn within the first year, but the thought of one day hurting them more than they could ever hurt me kept me going.

"You wanted this. You wanted to be a part of this world, and yet, every damn time"—he slammed his hands against the table and pushed his chair back with a skin-crawling screech—"maybe you're not cut out for this life, given your inability to follow orders."

One time Sawyer didn't treat me any differently from the boys was when angry fists were flying.

"Got it," I said dryly, choosing not to push my luck too far in one day. It wasn't the run I wanted, but damned if I could turn it down.

Fuck someone over, then fuck the new guy. It was simple enough. Or so I thought.

# She-Devil: Chapter Two

---

## DEVIL WITHOUT A CUT

### Trent

I WAS in over my head. Over the head of anyone involved in this shanty operation, which was becoming larger and more complex at every turn.

We'd all dreamed of finally bringing justice to the rogue motorcycle gang, but my assignment didn't start out that ambitious. Over the last few months, a series of fentanyl overdoses linked to rape cases in Ashville had gotten a little too close to home, taking the life of a fellow detective who'd been investigating the case. Then, a tip led me to Bone Grinders, a repair shop on the outskirts of Ashville known as The Point, or more locally, Devil's Point. A place cops and well-informed citizens avoided at all costs because it was the territory of the Devils of Ashville Motorcycle Club. I didn't imagine their acronym was DOA by chance.

The Club was a rising threat to the area, a tight-knit community with a well-established foundation, and they didn't even try to hide their involvement in drugs, guns, murder, or robbery. They didn't have to. And despite all that, the authorities had yet to catch a break that would shake the club to its core.

The club navigated the legal minefield as if they had detailed maps of every plan the police in the district came up with, raising suspicions that they had hooks in someone on the inside. Someone who gave them enough info to change their plans at the last minute and outmaneuver officers at every turn. Chief Lewis and Captain Ainsley then decided to bring in someone from another district—me—to get eyes on the ground. Few enough of the local police would know me on sight, and it helped that I looked more like a biker than a detective. The list of those who knew about this rogue operation was short; the chief and Captain Ainsley, as well as my captain, my partner, and Officer Ryan Corell, who was acting in my place as James's partner during my temporary reassignment. Which left me with few options if I needed backup.

I had only intended to hang around the shop long enough to find out if someone from the group was involved in the overdoses and catch the cop who might be feeding them information. But I stumbled into something deeper when Cannon, the Club's VP, offered me a job at the shop. Half of the workers were heavy drinkers and addicts: meth, heroin, coke. And there was plenty to go around. Others had only the slightest competence in repairing a bike. They were only around to collect a paycheck. Cannon and his son-in-law, Caine, were the only ones who seemed to have the slightest clue what they were doing. And in truth, they were good mechanics, and with my lifetime of tinkering and rebuilding nearly every type of vehicle, they were eager for me to step in and help.

Chief Lewis agreed to let me continue and made the

necessary arrangements for the infiltration. The opportunity was too good—even though we didn't have the resources for a full undercover investigation, that's what it had turned into. We were already in unprecedented territory with the club.

With the official job offer, came the necessity of cementing my undercover identity. A new ID, bank account, shitty apartment—whatever I could get my hands on. The connections that James and I had made when he was under at The Retreat helped, but we were still working with a skeletal framework.

I don't know what our knack for getting close with the bad guys says about me or James, but here I was, one run away from official Prospect with the Devils of Ashville Motorcycle Club. Everyone in this part of town would soon see me as a Devil. An unpredictable outlaw with the temper of lit pine pitch.

I trailed behind Caine as we descended the stairs from Sawyer's office to the bar below. The Devil's hangout was located in a refurbished opera house of all places. When the steel industry moved away from The Point, the area wealth took a nosedive. The void left the perfect opportunity for groups like the Devils to take hold, grow, and prosper.

From the bar, Caine led me through a side door marked MEMBERS ONLY and into a smoky room where the club usually gathered for church. The long wooden table in the center of the room was lined with guns and ammunition, so I assumed the men present were gearing up for something serious.

"Guys." Caine tipped his head to the crowd of men gathered around. "This is Trent from the shop."

One guy snorted. "Looks like you took a wrong turn."

Another stepped out of the corner, cracking his knuckles. He was round and bushy like a Biker Santa, and as I recalled his name was Fitch, Caine's father. Also known to the club as The Wise One. He and Sawyer would play a large role in my continued association with the club—or my demise if I fucked this up.

"Used to be with the Brotherhood, right?" Fitch asked.

"Nothing official. My uncle rode with them. I was too young to join up."

"Uncle have a name?" another asked. I knew him as Gavin—or "Vin" among his friends. He frequented the shop to do—well, fuck up would be a more appropriate term—his own repairs, and usually ignored my presence entirely. His black, curly hair was slicked back and clung to the sides of his head so tightly it looked like a tacky, faux mullet.

"Vic 'Hawg' Clevenger." A real member of the Brotherhood. Although he'd died about twenty years earlier when the members of the club turned against each other, leading to a string of murders and violence.

"Hawg?" Fitch's eyes narrowed. "Whatever happened to that Softail of his?"

A subtle and carefully laid trap. "Didn't know he ever had one. He loved his custom Wide Glide though."

Fitch didn't respond. He merely leaned back into his corner and took a long drag from his cigarette.

The others, however, weren't so easily appeased.

"You must've made some deal with the Devil to escape that mess," Gavin said.

"He's a brother looking for a new home," Caine interrupted. He sounded forceful but wore his tension in shifting his weight from foot to foot. I'd seen it enough times to know.

"Not our brother yet," Gavin said.

I had to walk a treacherous fine line. Too much of a pushover and they'd never respect me or take me seriously, bit if I overstepped the bounds too much, the results would be just as bad. I cocked my head. "Then, why am I doing a job for the club? Does Sawyer not trust you assholes any more than a stranger off the streets?"

I knew that comment would tick them all off, but I chose to get it over with. I had to be brash, cocky, and confident, goading them into making the first move.

A man to my right charged toward me, throwing a punch, but I ducked and elbowed him in the gut. In standing my ground, I chose each maneuver carefully to keep the damage minimal. "I'm not here to cause trouble in the club."

The next attacker's punch came at me low, so I stepped aside and kicked out his knees, bringing my elbow down against the back of his neck as he stumbled.

The first man swung at me again, his fist connected with my jaw, but I grabbed his forearm and twisted until he went to his knees as well. "Is this necessary?"

"The Wheel fell because they trusted the wrong person," Fitch said, still puffing his cigarette lazily in the corner. "You understand our concern."

"Concern?" I stepped back as both men who'd attacked me straightened. "Looks a lot like animosity to me."

An arm tightened around my neck blocking my airway while the first two threw an additional punch each.

"Boys." A female voice filled the room. "If you can stop playing, we have work to do."

"Well, get to it, Mama," the man with his arm around my neck said—I then recognized his voice as Gavin.

"You're holding up my—" I watched her jaw pulse.

"Trent is with me tonight. We have a long ride to the Grove. Not to mention, you have your own run to get ready for, so fuck off and don't hold me up."

The arm around my neck loosened, but they weren't about to take orders from a woman, even if she did outrank most of the men in the room. Their reluctance was written all over their condescending scowls and wide stances. Instead, everyone in the room looked to Gavin, who suddenly released me and shoved me forward.

Before I could regain my balance, Brooke punched me in the shoulder blade. "Move, Prospect."

No one ever said this experience would be pleasant.

She directed me to a large walk-in closet at the back of a room, jerked a coat off the wall, and chucked it at me.

"It's not going to fit," I said. It was far too straight and narrow and would never fit over my shoulders.

She gave me a flat look. "Slim pickens 'round here, it seems."

But from where I stood, there seemed to be several options. "You want me to rip the arms out?"

Her lips turned white and a deep growl rumbled in her chest. "Do it, and I'll rip yours off."

The other guys didn't seem to fear her, but from where I stood, she had more than an ounce of intimidation in that small frame. Her leather jacket and dark jeans were fitted to her tall, athletic figure, and her hair cascaded down her back with a slight wave as if she'd had it tied up. The right side of her head was shaved, a harshness mirrored in her choice of makeup.

I put my arm through the sleeve to demonstrate. "Ain't happenin,' honey."

She ripped it out of my hands and jerked me forward by

the collar of my shirt. "Get this, Prospect, I'm neither yours no anyone's honey, baby, Ol' woman, sugar, or darling. I'm the Club Treasurer and I didn't get my patch through some honorary bullshit. Try that shit on me again and you'll lose more than your manhood."

*Goddamn.* I held my hands in the air. "All I'm asking for is a leather that fits. I have to be able to move."

I reached past her for another coat that looked to be about my size, but Brooke knocked my hand away. "Not. That. One."

"You're damn fussy about a piece of dead cow skin."

With a growl, she ripped another off the hook and chucked it at me. This one looked like it'd fit Fitch if he gained forty pounds.

"Are you serious right now?" I had expected a hard time, but this was downright petty.

Caine opened the door, joining us in the tight space. He scratched the hair at his temple—another of his tells. "What's—?"

"Fuck off, Caine. I'm picking up where you obviously failed."

"Really?" He eyed the coat in my hand and groaned. Then, he yanked down the coat Brooke had gotten all fussy over and handed it to me.

Brooke huffed and stormed out.

"What the fuck?" I asked, keeping my voice low so only he could hear.

Caine stared at the door. "Looks like Sawyer has decided to throw you to the rabid wolf."

"Not exactly the answer I was looking for." I shrugged on the jacket, pulling the hood of my shirt over the collar.

He squinted at me over his shoulder. "That leather

belonged to her brother. He disrespected the club and was stripped of it three years ago."

My stomach flipped with the not-so-subtle affirmation that this was going to be a shit day.

Maybe I should've just accepted the over-sized throw-rug for a jacket.

# She-Devil: Chapter Three

## DEVIL IN BLUE JEANS

### Brooke

I AVOIDED LOOKING at Trent for as long as possible while we prepped our bikes for the ride. The Salt Grove was a good two hours away—if you did the speed limit. Lonnie and Sawyer had been doing business for a long time, but after some prying from Lonnie's wife, he moved up north to get out. He failed to consider that once you do business with the Devil, he never lets go, and a two-hour drive wouldn't make a difference when reckoning came around.

I twisted my hair up and tucked it under my helmet. When I turned to adjust my tail bag, I noticed Trent watching.

"Can I ask what this run is about?" he asked.

I groaned. "Prospects don't ask questions. Just follow me and do what I say."

With everything I might need tucked away, I yanked the zipper closed, and fastened the buckles on the leather flap. *Just get it over with. Deal with Lonnie. Fuck the Prospect.*

*Yeah, fucking right.*

Oh, I knew it would happen. I had every intention of following orders, and I always packed enough preventative measures to ensure it all went according to plan. A gun, a knife, and condoms—what order I used them in was yet to be determined. One thing I had learned from the men in the club, we didn't have to be nice to fuck.

And no one ever said any of it had to be pleasant.

Trent zipped up his leather jacket and straddled his bike. I almost dropped my keys and the instant pang of hurt it sent through me. *He shouldn't be wearing Dix's jacket.* The leather had been stripped of patches and identifying marks, but that didn't make it any different.

Sawyer was wrong.

He'd set out to shame my brother's name by stripping him of his colors and leaving his jacket around for any damn Prospect to pick up. Sawyer was wrong about a lot of things, but he was also too stupid and arrogant to realize it. His stubborn ignorance was the key reason my brother was no longer around. But since our President couldn't be wrong, of course it was Dix who disgraced the club.

I revved my engine, feeling the vibrations consume my body, and without a word, hit the throttle. This was where we separated brothers from men on bikes. Anyone who had never ridden a hog for two hours straight shouldn't be setting foot in our clubhouse in the first place.

Part of me hoped this guy's balls were so big they'd be ready to fall off by the end of the night and he'd have no interest in fucking. But Sawyer would blame me for that, too.

Instead of thinking about it, I rode hard and fast, using the open road as the only catharsis I could get. Even though I set a break-neck speed, Trent kept up. Around every curve, through every intersection, and past the cop tucked behind the billboard where he always waited. I wondered how tempting it might be for him to pick up a couple of Devils, but as usual, he didn't budge.

We reached The Salt Grove in just over an hour and found Lonnie's home in one of those cookie-cutter neighborhoods where each house looked almost exactly like the next. We parked our bikes behind a black SUV in the drive, and I removed my helmet, slinging it over a side mirror. Beside me, Prospect climbed off his bike—far too limber for a guy who'd ridden more than a hundred miles, at twice the speed limit. Sure, he looked like a guy who'd sat in the same position without a break on crumbling and winding roads, but he wasn't falling on his face stiff or walking like a man with a double-edged sword between his legs.

Much to my disappointment, but there was always the return trip.

"Plan?" he asked.

At least he seemed resolved to keep our conversation to a minimum. "Nope."

His stern expression faltered, but he took a step back and motioned for me to take the lead.

Maybe we could get along.

I walked around the house to the saddest back patio I'd ever seen—a single square of concrete with one half-dead plant. Back doors weren't as well-guarded or fortified, but Lonnie must've heard us coming and would've been stupid to leave it unlocked.

He wasn't stupid.

When the knob refused to turn, I stepped to the side, looking to Prospect. He raised an eyebrow and smirked, then kicked the perfect sweet spot to bust the fragile door jamb half off the wall. Sure, these cookie-cutter houses were expensive, but that was mainly due to the location, not the craftsmanship. Certainly the housing community would appreciate our improvements.

"You've done this before," I said.

He shrugged. "We can work on the mutual commendations later."

I had to get paired with the smart ass. I rolled my eyes and stepped past him and over the debris left in the doorway. My hand rested on the gun handle hidden below my jacket. The house was deathly quiet, and I expected Lonnie to be hiding, or not even there. But Sawyer didn't leave things to chance. He knew schedules, habits, and usually the darkest secrets.

Trent and I walked into the living room to find Lonnie sitting on the sofa with a remote resting on one knee and his cell on the cushion next to him. He was too calm.

The skin on the back of my neck prickled with the intense electric energy in the room.

"Lonnie." I tried to get a read on his threat level.

"It was only a matter of time," he said in an even tone. "At least you waited until Madeline was gone."

"Sawyer wants his money. Cash."

Lonnie scoffed. "Sawyer always wants something."

"Then pay and be done with it." I, for one, wanted this over as quickly as possible.

"Done with it?" he said with an ironic laugh as he stood. "Have you ever known anyone to be done with your father, or for him to let it go after all debts are paid."

*Only when they were dead.* Even then, he had a hard time letting anything go. But I wished Lonnie would just pay up. I was good at violence for anger's sake, beating the crap out of a man apparently resigned to his fate was a different story. It threw the situation off kilter, and I suspected that was his intent.

"Pay or things get dirty." I had to find a way under Lonnie's skin, and when I spotted a picture of Madeline on the mantel, I had an idea. "Sawyer sent us here to hurt you and make sure you get the message, but I'm thinking the best way to do that won't be breaking your kneecaps."

His eyes flashed as the composure faded from his face, certainly regretting what he'd said earlier. He should have gone with fear. Resignation only revealed his hand.

I stepped forward until we were chest to chest. "See, I'm all about equal opportunity and it seems Madeline should stand as an equal partner in this little deal."

Lonnie's eyes narrowed, focusing on me. His jaw was so tight, I could practically hear him grinding his teeth. "Leave her out of it."

"What is it she does?" My voice almost purred and I wasn't sure whether to be proud or disgusted.

Lonnie's lips turned white.

"Doesn't she run that little private STEM school in town. What if something were to happen? An accident followed by a failed drug test? Maybe some rerouted money. I'm sure no one would stand for that. Especially when they realize the diverted money is going to pay your illicit debt. She'd be ruined. And, well, we all know how you make your money, so good luck dealing with an even more furious Sawyer after that."

"That's a lot of your father's blood and anger running through your veins." Of course, he knew my weak spot too.

"Pay and we'll be done here," I repeated.

A reflection bounced off the walls around us, and Prospect pulled back the curtain to look out front. "A Cadillac SUV just pulled in."

I stiffened. Lonnie's phone had been right next to him. What if he'd called someone? What if he had backup?

But then, I saw even more panic in his eyes.

*Madeline is home,* I thought.

Either Sawyer had his information wrong, or he intended for Madeline to walk in on us laying out her husband.

"Decisions, decisions," I said as Lonnie watched the front door. *Would he have been so calm if he'd known she was coming home?*

"I'll get him the money." His voice rattled. "I don't have it here."

"Then, let's go get it," I said, grabbing between his legs and squeezing as the lock on the front door clicked.

He looked from the door to me. "I need a few days," he grunted.

I squeezed harder. "Wrong answer. Get the wife, Prospect."

Quick footsteps crossed the room behind me, the door opened, then Prospect gasped.

Lonnie sighed and the blood rushed out of his face.

"Brooke," Prospect said cautiously. I snapped my head around to find out what his ineptitude was about, but what I saw was a very, very pregnant woman.

And not Madeline.

"You have a pregnant fucking mistress? Getting into bed with Sawyer didn't teach you enough?"

Lonnie didn't make a sound, but behind me his mistress squeaked, "Derek? Who's Sawyer? What—"

"Shut up," Lonnie hissed.

"Well...." I grinned releasing my death grip on his junk and taking a step back. "I'm guessing we figured out where the money is. Does Madeline know about this?"

"No," he said.

"What's going on, Derek?" the mistress stuttered.

*And what is with this Derek bullshit?* He brought this woman into his house, knocked her up while photos of his wife sat on the mantel, and she didn't even know his name. I nearly choked on my breath. She had to be a fucking dimwit. And it turned out Lonnie was scum on a whole new level—not a surprising one.

"I need a few days," Lonnie hissed.

*Do we beat a man in front of a very pregnant and possibly ready to pop woman?* I couldn't say it would be the worst thing for her. She needed a reality check as much as him. Sawyer wouldn't care about her, only results. We sure as hell wouldn't go back empty handed.

"Not good enough." I punched him straight in the nose. He jerked back, blood running down the front of his shirt as he covered his face.

Also not good enough.

"Derek." Prego-mistress waddled forward until Prospect grabbed her arm.

"Love," I said, turning to her. I found terms of endearment the most condescending things known to man, and in this case, highly effective. "You should really—" I took a step toward her. "Really." Another step. "Get as far from this as possible before your little one becomes a pawn."

**Grab your copy…**
**vinci-books.com/skyshedevil**

# Acknowledgments

First and foremost, my gratitude goes out to my husband, who has never given up on me and supported me through the good and the bad. When I told him I wanted to start writing again, he never wavered and has encouraged me every step of the way. He goes out of his way to make sure I have dedicated writing time and insists that I stick to my goals. Our start to 2020 was particularly rough, but we made it through together, and I wouldn't know what to do without him by my side.

I also want to thank my family for never doubting or questioning my dream of being an author. I was encouraged from a young age to write, and my grandparents took me to the library regularly so I could always have a pile of new reading material. My 7th-grade English teacher, Mrs. Cook, encouraged me to write, enter competitions, and assured me that she believed I would be a published author one day. Despite my reluctance to reveal the nature of my books, having been raised in a conservative area, my family quickly offered their support and often talked about my books with friends and co-workers. I have been fortunate to have had a lifetime of encouragement, surrounded by individuals who embrace my work.

After joining the online author community, I discovered many friends who shared my lifelong dream and readers who are always eager to support my career and my work. Many have become lifelong friends. Pepper Winters and

Lyra Parish were among the first people I truly connected with. Pepper's friendship and guidance have meant the world to me over the last seven years. We spent almost every day writing together for many years, and we probably talked to each other more than our spouses some days. Lyra is simply an amazing person, and her willingness to help others and support the writing community inspires me every day.

My first readers, Sasha, Sheila, Becca, Vicki, Amber, and LK, have also provided a source of strength and resilience for me. These amazing ladies have always been there to provide words of encouragement, critiques, and catch the silly errors that have slipped through the net. I appreciate them putting up with my insanity and willingly acting as the guinea pigs for all of my work.

Finally, thank you to every reader who makes it possible to keep following my dreams. I hate doing acknowledgments because I always feel like there is someone who is going to be left out, but every person who has encouraged, supported, and interacted with me over the last seven years will always be in my heart because you have made this journey a little easier, a little more entertaining, and worth every moment of struggle.

## About the Author

Skye Callahan is a bestselling author who enjoys writing fiction to explore the darker aspects of human nature and the resiliency needed to survive and overcome difficult situations. She hopes to show that even through the darkest moments and overwhelming circumstances, one can find the inner strength to adapt and eventually heal.

Skye lives in the hills of Appalachia with her husband and their feline overlords: Sassy, Knight, Raith, Dresden, and Crowley, and enjoys hanging out in the yard with all the natural wildlife (except rattlesnakes). When she's not reading or writing, she might be found in the garden, watching horror movies, or playing video games with the hubs. Prior to pursuing writing full-time, Skye earned an M.A. in History and participated in numerous local history projects, including a full-length Civil War documentary for PBS.